The Gemini Bond

Celina Pavan

This is a work of fiction. Names, characters, places, and incidents are the product of the author's imagination and are used fictitiously. Any resemblance to actual events, locales, or persons, living or dead, is coincidental.

Cover design by: Arturo Barraza, Artezuma Studio
email: arturobarraza75@yahoo.com

Published by:
Solfeggio Publications, LLC
Glendale, Arizona

Copyright © 2011 Celina Pavan
email: celinapavan@hotmail.com
website: www.geminisouls.com

All rights reserved. This book may not be reproduced in whole or in part, or transmitted in any form, without written permission from the author and/or publisher, except by a reviewer who may quote brief passages in a review; nor may any part of this book be reproduced or transmitted in any form or by any means electronic, mechanical, photocopying, recording, or other, without written permission from the author and/or publisher.

ISBN: 978-0-9838138-1-1

ACKNOWLEDGMENTS

Writing is said to be a solitary pursuit, but I found it was never lonely. I was blessed with a great many friends, guides, and advisors who made my task not only easier, but also better in every way. I am grateful to each and every person. This is their book as much as mine.

I wish to extend my heartfelt thanks:

To Mayor Adolfo Gamez, who imparted insights into public service and the unique challenges of leadership in a small community.

To Alana Bottinelli and Misty Reyes, who supplied details of the duties and responsibilities of a human services aide and social worker.

To Barbara, Jenn, Stephanie, Connie, and Amy, who reviewed earlier drafts of the manuscript and provided valuable feedback.

To Patricia Peters of A Word Affair, who offered her excellent suggestions for improving the story and enhancing the characters.

To Arturo Barraza, who listened to my ideas for the book cover and created something truly artistic.

To Wanda F., who provided background on the airplanes that are on display in various parks around Phoenix, and who tendered a sympathetic ear during the Great Computer Catastrophe.

To the Monthly Lunch Quartet, who kept my spirits up and made me laugh on numerous occasions (and still do).

To Stephanie M., who doesn't think I'm any more crazy than she is, and who has bestowed her unique wisdom on several occasions.

To Barbara B., who slogged through the manuscript not once, but *twice*, and has the eyes of an eagle for overlooked details. I am grateful for her support and friendship.

And, finally, to my husband, who is my rock, and who believed I could accomplish anything I deeply desired, even before I thought I could. I am truly blessed. *Grazie, amore.*

"There are more things in heaven and earth, Horatio,
Than are dreamt of in your philosophy."

- William Shakespeare
Hamlet, Act I, Scene V

"When you make the two into one, and when you make the inner as the outer, and the upper as the lower, and when you make male and female into a single one, so that the male shall not be male, and the female shall not be female: . . . then you will enter [the kingdom]."

- Jesus
The Gospel of Thomas, Saying 22

CHAPTER 1

The boy could hear his father's voice even before he slammed his way into the apartment. As footsteps approached the front door, he and his mother locked eyes. He gave a quick glance to the calendar hanging from the thin nail on the kitchen wall. Underneath "April" were big red X's running through two of the Friday dates. One was today. *It's payday,* the boy realized. *Papa bought a bottle to celebrate.*

His mother pushed herself out of the kitchen chair and began rummaging through the cupboards for cans of food. The boy watched his mother, feeling tense and unsure of what to do.

The front door slammed closed. "Hey, what's for dinner?" bellowed the father.

The mother bit her lip. "I'm getting it ready right now," she said in a tremulous voice. "Go ahead and wash, and I'll have it ready for you in a bit."

The boy jumped as his father's huge body appeared at the kitchen entrance. The man's work clothes were smeared with mortar stains and dirt. He took a long swig from the tequila bottle. He twisted the cap on the bottle crookedly and swayed on his feet as he wiped his mouth with his stained long sleeve.

"You, boy, what are you doing there? Just sitting around, doing nothing?"

The boy stood, motioning to his mother. "No, I was going to help Mama with the table." He stood protectively between the hulking man and his mother.

The father pushed the boy out of the way. "So, woman, what are you fixing for me tonight?" He smacked her hard on the rear. He laughed, spewing drops of foul-smelling saliva. The mother froze, her eyes filled with fear.

The father took another gulp from the bottle and noticed the two pairs of eyes locked on him. He swore and hit her hard on the back, between the shoulder blades. The mother gasped as she grabbed the stove to steady herself.

"Get to work, woman! I'm a hungry man!" His wife remained motionless.

"You lazy pig! Get to work or you'll be sorry!" He slammed the bottle on the kitchen table. "You lazy fat slob! Move it!" He punched her with his giant fist in the solar plexus. She fell to one knee, coughing and clutching her stomach.

The boy jumped in front of his father. He put up his hands to block any more blows aimed at his mother.

"You little flea," his father roared. "Get out of my way."

The boy stood his ground, his mouth tight and his eyes flashing. "Stop this, Papa. Leave her alone. You're drunk and you're being a bully."

The father's eyes narrowed as he found a new target. "You worthless bastard. You are a lazy good-for-nothing, just like her." At that, his fists became blurs as they rained blows on the boy's body, starting with his torso, and, as the boy fell to the ground, coughing and moaning, feet kicked him in the stomach, in the back, on his thighs. All the while, the father continued to roar curses at his son. The father stepped over the prone boy and finished venting his anger on his wife. The sounds of her body being pummeled mixed with her screams and moans doubled the boy's agony.

Finally, the father wandered off to the bedroom with his bottle in hand. Curled in a ball, crying and coughing up bile, he knew he could not live here any longer. He glanced at his mother, crumpled on the floor, the back of her hand pressed to her mouth as she tried to stifle her sobs.

I'll find a way to help my mother and brothers, he swore to himself. *Someday. Somehow.*

CHAPTER 2

Clarissa Wright, called Rissa by her friends, put the window visor down to cut the glare of the early June sun. The chipper weather forecaster on the morning news report said that it could be a record-beating high temperature for Denver. The news caused Rissa to sigh. *Lucky me, I get to drive around this crazy traffic in my old un-air-conditioned car,* she thought. *I guess I'll just roll down the windows and drive fast.*

She was making a home visit to a mother whose child had been removed due to neglect. Two-and-a half-year-old Jazmin, fussy in the car seat as Rissa drove, already had experienced too much in her short life. A couple of months back, she had been found toddling alone in the middle of the street, and was nearly hit by a garbage truck doing its early morning run. She was filthy and ill and tests showed drugs in her system. The courts took her away and placed her in a foster home, where Rissa picked her up over a half hour ago. Rissa's job was to supervise the visits between the mother, fresh out of rehab and working part time, and the child. How these meetings went would determine if and when the mother and child could be reunited for good.

Rissa parked in a spot marked for visitors and sighed. She was thinking of a phone call some weeks prior with her father, discussing her new job as a human resources aide. Her father was of the firm opinion that his daughter, if she was determined to work in this kind of job, should start at the level of a case manager, not a lowly aide.

"But Dad, I'm still working on my degree and they won't hire me for a higher position until I've completed it. This job gives me all sorts of experience to put on my resume and," she added in a softer voice, knowing he wouldn't understand, "it makes me feel like I'm making a difference."

"But you need to be in charge. You're too good to be wiping babies' butts as you tote them around to no-good parents. People don't really change. I've seen it over and over again. You're wasting your time."

Rissa held her breath for a moment and let it out through pursed lips. She and her father had been over this territory before. He didn't approve of her choice of a career, working with difficult family situations, enduring low pay, and garnering little respect. He'd always hoped that she would follow his footsteps in becoming an attorney, and eventually take over his small but profitable law office. He couldn't understand her need to show people the way out of their misery, to cheer them into better lives and healthier habits, and to see broken relationships mended. The phone call ended, as it always did, with cordial but not heart-felt goodbyes.

Rissa peered into the rearview mirror to give herself a quick once-over. Her straight, shoulder-length hair, a sable-brown color that kids in grade school had compared to the color of their classroom pet rat, was fastened into a neat ponytail. She flicked at her bangs, making sure that they covered her birthmark, a roughly almond-shaped patch an inch and a half above her left eye which was about two shades darker than her normal skin tone. When she was young, she asked her mother what it was. Her mother kissed her and said, "It's the place where God kissed you, honey. Don't be afraid to show it." A couple of months later, Rissa's mother had been killed by a drunk driver, pinned against the wall of the Pay 'N Go drug store on Sixth Avenue as she was walking home after doing an errand. After that, Rissa grew tired of the cruel teasing of her second-grade classmates about her birthmark, so she always covered it with bangs. Since her mother's death, there had been no one in Rissa's life to make her feel special anymore, with her father busy with his law practice, and her grandmother stepping into her life only occasionally. *All I have is my invisible friend, and he's not even real,* she thought. Rissa sighed, shook her head, and continued the inspection. Hazel-brown eyes free of dangling eyelashes or crusty matter, check. Nothing hanging out of her nose, check. No salad remnants stuck between her teeth, check. She made a vain attempt at brushing off cat hair from her green tee shirt and black slacks, and exited the car. She glanced at her reflection in the car window, pulling the tee shirt down over her slender hips. *Good enough for an overworked twenty-two, I guess*, she thought.

Rissa opened the back door of the car to free Jazmin from the car seat. She balanced the toddler on her hip and held her notebook and purse in the other hand. With the hot weather and the car's lack of air conditioning, sweat made the child's dark hair curl even more. Rissa took a quick whiff to see if the baby's diaper needed changing before she went to see the mother, but the child seemed clean for now. She walked up the cracked sidewalk to the ground floor apartment, one among many in this run-down development. *Like rabbit hutches*, she thought. The small lawn in front of the building was sparse and weedy. It looked like it had not received much water during the recent hot spell. A lone juniper, bald of branches in the middle, leaned drunkenly toward the door. Rissa touched the pendant at her throat while taking a deep, steadying breath. She knocked, took one step back and slightly to the side.

The next-door neighbor's door swung open. "Are you Missy?" asked a woman's voice.

"Uh, Rissa."

"Uh-huh. Tina's runnin' late. She called me 'cause she lost your phone number. She missed her bus back from work but said she'll be here in ten or fifteen minutes. You can wait in here if you want to get out of the heat. Just give me a minute." The door closed.

Rissa stepped under the small porch which shielded the neighbor's door from the late-May sun as she considered her options. *Do I risk heat stroke for the baby as we wait here or in my car? Or do I trust a woman I've only seen a couple of times before and hope that my client shows up soon? Jeez, they don't teach you about this stuff,* she thought. She heard scuffling inside, like someone throwing papers and garbage around. An infant's wail from inside grew louder over the blare of the TV set. After a couple of minutes, the door swung open.

"Come on in." A large woman stood at the door, wobbling on two tree trunks for legs, her feet tucked into pink fuzzy slippers. Her hair color, a kind of pinkish red, was a shade not to be found in Nature, but from a box at the local grocery store. Her pasty white skin was mottled with red sores in various degrees of scabbing. Her yellow and green dress hung off one shoulder and Rissa could see from the tags peeking at the back that it was inside-out. The odors of beer and urine emerged like an acrid cloud.

"How long did you say it would be before Mrs. Ávila returned? We had a two o'clock appointment."

The woman swayed as she looked over her shoulder into the darkness within. "Oh, another ten minutes or so. You can stand out here in the heat or come inside. Your choice." She clucked as she looked at the child starting to fuss on Rissa's hip. "Goodness! Look at how much Jazmin has grown! She's getting bigger than my own boy."

Rissa bit her lip. She promised herself to leave after ten minutes. If Mrs. Ávila couldn't keep a court-ordered appointment, it would have to go into her report. Still, if there was a transportation problem, she wanted to give the woman a chance.

She stuck out her hand. "Clarissa Wright." The woman's handshake was sweaty and limp.

"Ginger Saenz. Please come in."

"Thank you, Mrs. Saenz." Rissa took one last lungful of fresh air before entering the apartment.

It took a minute for her eyes to adjust to the darkness inside. The windows were covered with tinfoil and one lone light bulb on a shadeless lamp glowed far in the corner of the room. Toys and papers lay in random piles on the furniture and floor; a garbage can in the kitchen overflowed with dirty diapers, beer bottles, and crusty tin cans. Flies orbited the pile of refuse. An unbalanced ceiling fan wobbled as it moved the air around in the room. Rissa tried not to let the distaste for the smell show on her face.

Mrs. Saenz cleared off a space on the sofa for Rissa to sit down. Rissa half-smiled and sat, secretly nodding to herself about the wisdom of never wearing something that she cared about while on the job. One of her mentors in college had taught her that, along with the notion of always wearing shoes that she could sprint in if things ever got rough.

Mrs. Saenz picked up her squalling child and tucked him under her arm while she pulled up a vinyl and aluminum chair from the kitchen. The boy wore only a sagging diaper; his nose was running and his dark hair was damp from sweat. His mother grabbed a bottle from the refrigerator and poked it into the boy's mouth before sitting. The crying stopped.

"Mind if we turn this down a bit?" Rissa reached over to the TV and turned down the volume. She knew better than to turn it completely off. In homes like these, it served as the only distraction from the ugliness of their reality. She sat the child in her care on her lap. The girl seemed content to watch the flashing images on the TV screen through drowsy eyes.

Rissa's practiced eyes scanned the other child for signs of neglect or abuse. He was free from bruises, of normal weight, and seemed content in his mother's arms. The condition of the apartment, while messy by Rissa's standards, did not seem to pose any immediate threat of harm to the child living here.

Rissa decided to see how much this neighbor knew of her client's progress. "So, Mrs. Saenz, how long have you known Mrs. Ávila?"

"Oh, we've both lived here quite a while now. We had our last babies at about the same time. This is Fernando – we call him Nino." She smiled at the boy in her arms who was sucking on a bottle half-filled with apple juice. "I've got two other boys. One's sixteen and the other's nine." She started rocking and chewing her lower lip. "They're both good boys, but the older one doesn't live here anymore. I miss him."

Rissa pointed to a family photograph on top of the dusty TV. "Is that their picture?" she asked.

"Yes, that's them. Manny's the one in the middle and Rigo's the older one. Rigo – that's short for Rigoberto – went to visit his grandmother in Phoenix in April and hasn't come back.

I don't think he will. He and his dad, they don't get along. Especially when his dad drinks, you know." She bit her lip. "He doesn't drink that much," she added quickly. "His dad is a good man, but sometimes things are hard for him at work. They take advantage at times. He gets mad. And that Rigo, he has a lip on him, you know? He didn't know when to shut up and sometimes his dad had to show him who's boss. He's not a bad kid." Nino was asleep now, his mouth agape and his head lolling with the motions of his mother.

"I see," said Rissa. She had learned that most families are dysfunctional in some way; her job was to focus on the most urgent cases. Still, her heart went out to this family torn apart by the rage of powerlessness and alcohol. She had seen it before.

A knock at the door showed that Rissa's client had arrived for her appointment. Rissa stood to leave, giving the child in her arms a gentle shake to wake up. Rissa thanked Mrs. Saenz, shook her damp hand again, and followed Mrs. Ávila next door.

Mrs. Ávila's apartment was tidier than she had ever seen it and she was pleased to hear that the mother was holding a part-time job on the cleaning staff of a downtown office building. Rissa spent some time watching them interact while writing her observations in her notebook containing files on her eleven current cases. Jazmin didn't seem comfortable with her mother, avoiding eye contact and pulling away when her mother tried to hold her. Worse yet, Mrs. Ávila's attempts to engage the child grew more and more forced each time the child pulled away. Rissa sensed the frustration and anger growing within the mother. Rissa worried whether they would be able to regain a bond. She felt the hope within her dim.

As she stepped into the sunshine of that summer day, she wondered again if she would ever make a good social worker. The feelings of hopelessness and buried anger clung to her inner being as much as the stench of the Saenz apartment stayed on her clothes. She had learned various techniques to get rid of those feelings, but she also knew that for her, there were days when those feelings were very difficult to dissipate. She needed a vacation.

She sat in her old Honda Civic, holding her breath for it to crank over and start, and laughed at the idea of being able to take a vacation. On her salary! It would take a miracle.

Little did she know that a miracle was on its way.

CHAPTER 3

Rodolfo Saenz was boiling with rage. He hated being taken advantage of and it had just happened again.

Yesterday, the boss at his new construction job pulled him aside as he was filling out his time card.

"Rudy, my boy, I have a friend who needs some light construction work in the basement of his house and I told him I knew just the man for the job." His boss, an overfed bull of a man, clapped Rodolfo on the shoulder. Rudy was eager to please his new boss. Even though he had been in this country since he was a toddler, without documents to prove his citizenship or a high school diploma, jobs were not easy to find.

Rodolfo agreed to contact the friend and arranged to come by his house this afternoon after work. He drove there in his old Ford pickup with a rusty muffler and parked. He was tired from a long day of hauling sheetrock into new housing construction. Still, the money would come in handy. He parked and sat for a minute, rallying his energy. Yes, the money would buy some new shoes for one of the kids and maybe a new dress for his wife. His fat, lazy wife. He hit the seat next to him. He married her when she was just seventeen, lithe and funny and pretty. But as she grew older, he found that she never could please him, except sometimes in bed. He urged her to take better care of the house, of the kids, of herself, but she was just fat and lazy. And he told her that, too. Maybe hearing it would make her change, but it didn't. Being in the apartment with her became a battle, with him trying to get her to do what he wanted, and her just cowering and doing nothing. Fat and lazy. Only his fists could move her now.

He walked to the house. The paper his boss handed him said the friend's name was Harry. He rang the doorbell and after a few seconds, Harry answered the door.

"You must be Rudy. Del has told me all about you, how you work real hard and need some dough, right?" Harry put his arm around Rodolfo's shoulder to usher him into the house and closed the door.

"The boss says you need work done in your basement, right? You show me what you want done?" Rodolfo was eager to get started and finish the job. No useless chatter for him.

They went to the basement, where Rudy saw that some water damage, probably from a poorly sealed basement window, had ruined some paneling on the wall and had warped some floor tiles. Harry explained that he needed Rodolfo to reseal the window, replace the paneling and the floor tiles and take the old stuff to the dump.

“How much are you going to charge me there, Rudy?” Harry bared his teeth in a semblance of a smile while his eyes betrayed an odd glint. Rudy pursed his lips while figuring the time and cost of materials, along with the gas to the dump and the dumping fee. He finally quoted a reasonable figure and Harry quickly agreed.

Rodolfo took some measurements, scribbled them on the paper his boss had given him with Harry's phone number on it, and went to the nearest home renovation store. He paid for the materials out of his gas and beer money, something he hated to do, but he knew it would be doubled soon enough.

The job took nearly two hours, and after Rodolfo loaded up the last of the old materials into the back of his truck, he knocked on Harry's door. It took a minute for Harry to answer.

"All finished. I'm ready to go to the dump now." Rodolfo stood at the doorway expectantly.

"Well, let's see here. You want cash, right? You don't want me to write a check that the government can trace, do you?" Harry licked his lips. The glint in his eyes was brighter.

"No, cash is good." Rodolfo extended his hand. Harry put a wad of bills in Rodolfo's hand. Rodolfo saw that the amount was half what he had quoted for the job.

"Mr. Harry, this is not right. This is not what we agreed."

Harry stepped outside of the house and stood chest to chest with Rodolfo. He peered down at the shorter man.

"Look here, you dirty Mexican illegal. You want me to call the immigration office? You want me to tell your boss so you lose your job? Take what you get and get out of here, you filthy bean-eater. Just go." With that, he turned his massive back and stormed in the house, slamming the door behind him.

Rodolfo stood for a minute with the money in his hand. After all that work, he just broke even. And he still had to go to the dump and pay the dumping fee. He felt a sickening sense of rage boil in his gullet.

He spit toward the door, turned on his heel and got in his car. He considered for a minute unloading all the trash from the back of his pickup onto Harry's lawn, but knew the man would probably call the cops on him. He started the car, put it into gear with a lurch, and squealed away. As he drove, the betrayals and cruelty of his life replayed in his mind. With each scene, the rage spread throughout his whole body until his brain felt feverish and his limbs afire. There was no way to get even, no way to win. And he knew that this was to be the story of his life.

After returning from the dump, Rodolfo stopped by the discount liquor store. He knew of no other way to quench the blaze of anger in his soul. He bought a couple of six-packs and a cheap bottle of tequila with the remaining cash in his pocket. He longed for some escape from this hopelessness.

By the time he was home, a quarter of the tequila bottle was empty. He found his wife staring blankly at the screen of the blaring TV while his youngest son, Nino, wailed in the corner of the room. His middle son, Manuel, was probably out with his friends.

"Where's dinner?" he bellowed.

His wife broke her fixed stare at the TV, suddenly aware that her husband was home. "Uh, I haven't started it yet. You said you'd be home late. We have beans and some peaches. That OK?" She got up and shuffled toward the kitchen.

He grunted and took another deep swig of tequila. He looked around at the mess of papers and toys strewn around the room. He kicked a couple of piles and picked up the squalling child.

"How's my boy?" he roared over the blare of the TV. Nino cried louder. "Hey, I think this kid's diaper is full. Why don't you take care of it?" he yelled to his wife.

"Um, I will, in a bit," she answered. He could hear the whine of the can opener and the rattle of pans as she prepared to heat the beans over the food-encrusted stove. He put the child down, sat in front of the TV, and opened a can of beer.

By the time dinner was ready, three cans of beer lay crushed at his feet. Rodolfo made a tipsy path toward the kitchen to be handed a plate of beans with cold tortillas. He took a bite, chewed once, and spit it out.

"These beans are cold, you lazy pig!" He grabbed the tequila bottle again and took a gulp. "You are a lazy, fat pig, a good-for-nothing wife and you can't even cook a decent meal!" He threw the plate of beans toward the sink. The child's wails grew frantic. "You can't even take care of the kids right! Where's Manny?"

"Rodolfo, don't do this. I wasn't feeling so good today. I got behind. Just settle down. The neighbors . . ."

"I don't care about the neighbors! Can't I come home to a decent meal for once? You drink your days away and don't care about anything else. Don't you think I've seen those bottles of booze in the trash? You're nothing but a lazy pig!"

With one swift motion, he kicked her, hard, on the upper thigh. He knew how to beat her so that no one would notice the bruises. She stumbled with a yelp, tripped on the kitchen rug and fell backward. Rodolfo was at her like a rabid wolf, kicking her on the thighs, in the stomach, and when she rolled over, in the kidneys. Her cries for him to stop only egged him on. He could no more stop the torments of his life than she could his violence. Even after she began gagging on vomit and blood, he kicked her once more, with vicious force, in the lower abdomen. She heaved a deep moan and was still.

Rodolfo looked around. He hated his life, he hated his home, and he hated what he was forced to do. The child's cries broke his concentration and he picked Nino up. "Stop! Stop! Shut up! Stop!" He shook the baby harder and harder, its head rolling back and forth like a rag doll's. Nino's wails were punctuated by hiccups of fear. "Stop!!" he yelled again, giving one last jolt to the baby's body. Nino's head snapped back and then lolled to the side as if he were asleep. The child was quiet at last.

Rodolfo took the tequila bottle to the bedroom and slammed the door. He would drown the remaining rage tonight and deal with his life tomorrow.

CHAPTER 4

"Clarissa, may I see you in my office?" Rissa's boss at the Department for the Protection of Children stood at the door of her office, her face stern.

Rissa's stomach tightened. She felt as if she were a naughty third-grader being summoned to the principal's office. Her supervisor often gave her the feeling that she disapproved of her, and found her work inadequate.

"Be right there." Rissa closed the file she was working on at her desk and made a mental note of where she needed to continue when she returned. She fingered her bangs, adjusting them as she walked. She took a deep breath and entered Mrs. Branson's office.

"Please close the door," said Mrs. Branson, and motioned for Rissa to sit down. She sat, holding her hands in her lap for fear of not knowing what to do with them.

"You were working on the Tina Ávila case, right?" Rissa nodded, although Mrs. Branson didn't look up for an answer.

She sat looking at a copy of the file and leafing through the notes that Rissa had made.

She continued. "I noticed that their address is very close to the apartment of a Mrs. Saenz. She has a couple of boys."

"Yes, actually, I met Mrs. Saenz yesterday. Mrs. Ávila was running a little late because she missed the bus, so she called Mrs. Saenz, who told me and had me wait inside her apartment." Rissa wondered frantically if that was against protocol. Still, it was a hot day and waiting in her little oven of a car wasn't really an option.

"You were inside the Saenz's apartment?" Mrs. Branson's pencil-thin eyebrows arched toward her hairline.

"Yes, it was hot and I didn't want to endanger the child in my care. Plus, my car's air-conditioning is broke again." She felt secure in her logic.

"Did you notice anything while you were inside the Saenz home?" Mrs. Branson locked her gaze on Rissa, who felt like the chair was sinking beneath her.

"Uh, no, not really. It was kind of messy and it smelled, but the little boy that I saw seemed well-fed and cared for." Rissa raised her eyebrows in a questioning look.

Mrs. Branson looked at Rissa for a long second, and then returned her focus to the file again. "No hints of abuse, violence, that sort of thing?"

Rissa sat up straighter, determined not to let the woman or the situation disempower her. "The mother, Mrs. Saenz, mentioned that the father sometimes had arguments with the oldest son, who left a couple of months ago. The mother looked pretty unhealthy and unkempt, but I didn't notice any bruises or anything. I didn't see any on the baby, either." She paused. "May I ask what this is all about?" She kept her face neutral, so as not to betray the growing annoyance she was feeling.

Mrs. Branson closed the file and pulled a paper from another pile on her desk. She referred to it as she spoke evenly, with as much emotion as she would have by reading from the local newspaper.

"Mrs. Saenz is in intensive care with multiple contusions, a ruptured spleen, and a perforated bowel. She's being taken care of at County Hospital. The nine-year-old, Manuel, found her when he got home last night about 8:30. He called 911. When the police came, they found the mother lying on the kitchen floor, the father passed out drunk in the bedroom, and the 10-month-old child dead of a broken neck. The father was taken to jail on suspected domestic violence and homicide. Manuel is now a ward of the state and was placed in foster care late last night." Mrs. Branson sighed through her nose, put the paper back down onto the appropriate pile, and once more stared at Rissa.

Rissa felt her face flush with sorrow and anger. "No," she whispered.

"Once word gets out that one of our human services advocates was in a home where this violence occurred, just a few hours before it happened . . ." Mrs. Branson's voice trailed off.

Rissa nodded, trying not to cry.

"I'll need a complete report of everything you saw, everything you said, and everything you heard, even if you were only there ten or fifteen minutes." Mrs. Branson cleared her throat. "I want that report completed before you leave today, Ms. Wright."

Rissa nodded again and left the office on shaky knees. She felt sick and wanted to be alone for a while. She sat at her desk, holding her head between her hands and closing her eyes. She sighed and told herself to focus on the task at hand.

She closed the computer file she had been working on and willed herself to relive the ten minutes she had spent in the Saenz apartment. She wrote with as much detail as possible, even including what type of food tins she saw in the trash.

That task completed, she finished writing up reports for a couple of other files, dropped off the Saenz file on her boss's desk ("Thank you, Ms. Wright," said her boss with her eyes glued to another report on her desk), and afterward left to make a couple of home visits in the afternoon. Those finished, she hand wrote some notes to be typed up tomorrow, closed her briefcase, and let her guard down.

At last, she could allow herself to *feel.*

Rissa entered her apartment on East 14th Avenue, dumped her keys and purse on a bookcase, threw herself on the bed and immediately burst into tears. Her three feline companions each greeted her in their own fashion: Sasha meowed nonstop, Regal primped, and Coco alternated between sniffing Rissa's hair and giving her head butts.

Rissa cried until she could cry no more. She got up, fed the cats, and thought about fixing herself some dinner. She searched her refrigerator and her cupboards and decided spaghetti with tomato sauce would do. She started up the water to boil and emptied the last of the tomato sauce from a glass jar into a pan to be heated. She felt a twinge of guilt doing so. Her Italian grandmother, if she ever saw this, would huff and scold her for eating sauce out of a jar. Rissa argued in her mind that there never seemed to be enough time to cook from scratch; besides, she didn't like to cook that much. She poured herself a glass of red wine to sip while cooking. The pasta ready, she put it into a colander to drain, poured it on a plate, and topped it with the ready-made sauce. She was looking around for some grated Parmesan cheese when the phone rang.

"Rissa? It's Carly. Hey, I heard what happened at work today. Oooh -- that's tough. How are you holding up?"

Rissa's friend from work, a relative old-timer in the office, was an unusual mixture of warmth and self-absorption. She was the type of person who would show people all her vacation photos, tell them her funny stories, but never ask anyone else what they did during their time off. Rissa thought of her as another person needing a listening ear, but not a true soul friend.

"Hey, Carly. Thanks for asking. I'm done crying, so it's got to be better from here, right?"

"Hey, you know, I had a case like that a couple of years ago. The boss made me cover the Department's butt, and she was a real hard ass about it, but we got through it OK. I told you about that, didn't I? The case where the kid was left unsupervised in the wading pool and almost drowned?"

"Yeah, you told me. I just feel like I'm expected to be psychic or something and be able to tell which cases might turn out bad and which ones will work out all right."

"Well, being psychic would definitely help. But for those of us who are not, it's better to just take really good notes and write good reports. I've seen your work, though. You do a pretty good job at that."

Rissa paused and said, "I just don't know if I'm cut out for this kind of work. I want to make a difference, but I just feel that I spend more time writing reports and protecting the Department than I do actually guiding clients. And when something like this happens . . ." Rissa sighed, " . . . it just tears me up inside. I don't see how you can keep your emotions out of it."

Carly was thoughtful for a minute. "Well, doll, just keep telling yourself that you're the guide, not their savior. Their decisions are all their own. There's really nothing you can do beyond that."

"OK, thanks," said Rissa, not feeling she received the answer she needed.

"Listen. I'll be in the office tomorrow morning. Will I see you there? Yes? Great. I'll check with you then. I have some new photos of the kids. Bye."

Rissa hung up the phone and contemplated her now cold and congealed pasta. She put it into the microwave for a minute, ate a few gluey bites, and threw the rest down the sink. She wasn't all that hungry, anyway.

Rissa slumped on the sofa and decided to quiet her thoughts with some deep breathing exercises. It took more time than usual, but she eventually reached a place of stillness. She allowed her imagination to lead her to a beautiful tropical garden, with pink and yellow hibiscus and tall date palms surrounding her as she sat on some lush, cool grass. She imagined how the air would smell sweet with flowers and ocean air, how the wind would blow gently through her hair, and how the sun would caress her cheeks with warmth. At that moment, as if from another room, she heard a piano playing. It came to her without her thinking about it first. Some gentle chords played one-two-three, one-two-three. A waltz. A delicate melody appeared that soared and pondered, whispered and announced, pushed and caressed. She recognized the style from her college music appreciation class. Chopin. A Chopin waltz. She didn't listen to that sort of music and didn't recall ever hearing this particular piece before, but she did not resist its beauty. Perhaps this was a gift from her invisible friend.

Rissa's mind wandered a bit. She recalled a classmate in first grade who played with an invisible friend, and Rissa remembered being slightly jealous of her for having such an ever-present and imaginative companion. As she grew older, however, Rissa realized that invisible friends were for lonely people, and she pitied the girl. Her mind traveled to when she was seventeen and had bumped her head after falling out a tree and developed a mild concussion; after that, Rissa noticed that her psychic abilities increased enormously. She not only felt what others felt emotionally, but she also could sometimes hear their thoughts. Soon after, she began seeing scenes in her mind's eye, as if looking at a snapshot taken from another's eyes – the inside of a desk drawer, a child's toy lying in the street, a moon peeking behind tall palm trees. She recalled how she felt emotions from this person, and she decided it was one person, not several people, because of the particular feeling, or vibration, she received – unique, like a psychic fingerprint. Sometimes it was a sudden burst of joy, making her want to thrust her hands to the sky and skip around the room, sometimes it was a deep sense of frustration, causing her to want to take a brisk walk or pound her fist into a pillow. Over time, she learned to shake the feelings off by acknowledging them and letting them go. Still, she treasured those connections she shared with her invisible friend. *Perhaps I'm just as lonely as that girl in first grade,* she thought. She shrugged and refocused. The music grew louder in her mind.

She smiled to herself, and then surrendered to the delicate embrace of the music.

CHAPTER 5

The morning sun broke through the shades of Rissa's bedroom window. She felt it would be a better day. She could hear the strains of the waltz in the back of her mind, like echoes of a distant romance. She laughed to herself. Romantic messages from someone who probably was a figment of her imagination! Not likely. She put the notion out of her head and busied herself with getting ready for work.

She made a home visit before going to the office. A little before ten, Carly found her busy at her desk, writing up reports from the morning visit and the visits from yesterday afternoon.

"Doll, don't you ever answer your messages?" said Carly.

"Oh. I think I've got my cell phone turned off. Why?" Rissa wasn't interested in hearing about the latest amazing thing that Carly's kids had accomplished. She wanted to finish her paperwork and get on with the day.

"They've finally called us! The Burly Bill and Breakfast Bob show on the radio has been calling your name for the last hour!

We're going to Hawaii if you get off your butt and call them before ten this morning!" Carly grabbed Rissa's desk phone and thrust it in her hands.

Carly read her the numbers while Rissa dialed. This was probably all a mistake. Her tone flat, she talked to the receptionist at the radio station and as it became clearer that it wasn't a mistake, Rissa's voice grew more and more animated. After a couple minutes, she was put through to the radio hosts.

"This is Burly Bill . . ."

" . . . and Breakfast Bob . . ."

" . . . .Wishing you good morning!" they both chimed. Their over-animated voices usually irritated Rissa, but this time she overlooked it. She was trying to remember when she had submitted her business card to the radio station, and recalled it had been a few months ago. Carly had made her promise that if either one won, they'd take the other on the trip.

The voices continued. "You're our winner to the last-minute trip to Hawaii. You and one friend will be going to the tropical islands of Hawaii IF you can answer one simple question." A dramatic pause.

Rissa cleared her throat. "Sure, what's the question?"

"Are you able to leave this Friday night for your fun-filled summer vacation to our fiftieth state?"

Rissa thought for a second. "You mean, in three days?" she asked.

"That's right! If you can leave Saturday, you and a special friend will enjoy an all-expenses-paid seven days, six nights trip to the beautiful Marquis Hotel on the island of Oahu, near Waikiki beach. Air fare for two is included, of course. So, what's your answer?"

"Just a minute." Rissa covered the phone with her hand and relayed the dilemma to Carly, who bolted for Mrs. Branson's door. Rissa considered for a minute. She was sure that Mrs.

Branson had read Rissa's report and passed it on to the caseworker. In case of a lawsuit, the caseworker was almost always called in to testify, even if their testimony was based on a lowly aide's report. Human service aides did not qualify as expert witnesses, and the Department would not want to risk having their aide's testimony discounted in court. Mrs. Branson would probably require Rissa to meet with the caseworker to go over her report, but otherwise would be happy to have her unavailable for a while in case the press came around, asking questions. Thirty seconds ticked by. Rissa uncovered the phone. "Um, we're asking the boss."

"No problem!" she was assured.

Another thirty seconds ticked by when Carly's head peaked out from Mrs. Branson's office. She gave a thumbs up sign, grinning broadly.

"It's OK! I guess we're cleared to go," said Rissa.

She was transferred to the receptionist again, who gave her the details about where to pick up the airline tickets and how to find the hotel. Her head swam with the suddenness of it all. She preferred plenty of notice to adjust to changes in her life. Still, she couldn't turn down a free vacation. She started making a list of all the things she needed to do – arrange for a cat sitter, get the suitcases out of storage, pack – and forced herself to calm down. By that time, Carly was squealing by her desk, "We're going to Hawaii! Doll, this is going to be great! Seven days without kids and hubby! Watch out, Hawaii!" She hugged Rissa's shoulders and danced off to her desk on the other side of the office. Rissa vowed not to let Carly get on her nerves. Nobody was going to ruin this vacation. She needed it.

CHAPTER 6

Rigoberto sat under a mesquite tree, studying the sky through the crisscross of branches. It was only ten o'clock, yet his grey tee shirt was already sticky on his back and beads of sweat dotted his forehead underneath his short but thick, black hair. He squinted, his eyes as dark as coal, looking for any sign of clouds that might bring rain later in the afternoon, but the sky's clear blue mocked his wish. He let his eyes lose focus and enjoyed how the branches above him lost their distinction and became a web of connections punctuated by blue emptiness. He sighed, wondering when his grandmother would return from the grocery store.

He wiped a trickle of sweat running down his cheek and considered going inside. Noises coming from the other trailers in the park and the whining of air conditioners showed that his grandmother's neighbors were staying inside until sundown. Desert dwellers, he was learning, adjusted their schedules according to the season. In the hot months, they arose early, did their outside chores and errands, and then stayed inside until sundown. Rigoberto hadn't adjusted his internal clock to this habit yet, and hated being cooped up all day. His grandmother's trailer felt claustrophobic to him, and he often felt that he was in her way.

Soon, the shrill whine of his grandmother's car roused him. The engine suffered from a loose belt, but his grandmother lacked the money to fix it. The clatter of tires on gravel stilled as she put the car into park and shut off the engine. A couple of blue puffs of smoke billowed from the tailpipe as the car sputtered and died.

"Help me, *mijo*, with these bags, OK?" said his grandmother.

Rigoberto stood and brushed the dust off his denim shorts. "Sure, OK." He grabbed two of the heavier bags and followed his grandmother into the darkness of the trailer. He still had to remind himself not to walk too heavily, as the floor gave with each step and sometimes the trailer bounced when he forgot he wasn't walking on a cement foundation. His grandmother scurried to close all the curtains in the trailer, shutting out all sunlight and heat. She switched on the light above the stove, which emitted an eerie yellow glow as she put her groceries away.

Rigoberto moved out of the way so as not to block her efficiency. He studied her, thinking back to the circumstances which brought him to live with this woman.

She was named Rosa for her mother's favorite flower, she once told him. She was a small woman, given to wearing the old-fashioned clothes of her home country, usually a boxy skirt with a knit blouse untucked at the waist. Her shoes were never fashionable, and alternated between the brown flat sandals she wore today and the scuffed leather shoes she wore when she went to Mass. Her hair, heavily grey, was pulled tight in a bun at the back of her head. Her one concession to dressing up was the string of pearls she wore about her neck when she attended church. Rigoberto wondered if they were real pearls. He considered for a moment, and decided they probably weren't.

She was his father's mother, having crossed the border almost thirty-five years ago, when her father was a toddler. She never talked about the crossing, but Rigoberto had heard whispers from others in the family that it was a horrifying experience, and that others in their group had died along the way. Rigoberto wondered how this small woman carried a young child while walking for days through the desert.

Some said that she came alone, except for the child with her, to escape a brutal marriage. Her husband had beat her and spit on her, they said. Rigoberto knew better than to ask her about the past. His grandmother's great strength was to live in the moment, to do whatever was necessary to get through the day, to put food on the table, and to help her family. She lived in Tucson for many years, raising her son and making ends meet by cleaning houses and later by working as a maid in the posh resorts. Although her English had improved over the years, she was hired less for her language skills and more for her work ethic, her reliability, and her tidy appearance. Her employers never questioned her lack of legal papers, but hired her because she was willing to work for less money than the native workers.

So she built her life and raised her boy, and learned the local language and ways by helping her son with his homework. Still, she enjoyed the *telenovelas* on TV and when the radio in her car worked, she would turn it to the Spanish language station to listen to the *ranchera* tunes of her home country.

Her son grew up to be an angry man, she believed, because of a lack of a father and because she was working such long hours. He had trouble in school and it seemed he spent more time home on suspension than in attendance. He never did graduate from high school and learned how to work in housing construction. He met a saucy, red-headed girl when he was eighteen and married when they found out she was pregnant. When Rosa saw that the girl was lazy and unable to keep a decent house for her son, she came to live with the young family and moved with them when they relocated to Denver to follow the construction jobs. She continued to work cleaning houses and hotel rooms, and tried to provide a stable home life for her son and his growing family. Over the years, she felt as if she were the last thread holding the unraveling family together, as anger and booze worked to rip it apart. Finally, she had a small heart attack and her doctor warned her that she needed to leave the stressful situation and go to a place where the high altitude and thin air would not tax her heart so much. She moved close to some cousins she had in Phoenix over a year ago and had been making ends meet with odd cleaning jobs and frugal living.

Rigoberto recognized in her a stability that his own home lacked, and when his father hit him one too many times, he borrowed some money from some friends and took a bus to Phoenix to live with her. He had been here for nearly three months, tried to make friends in his new high school during the last few weeks of the school year, and had yet to find his niche. In this small trailer, he felt like he was crowding her and taxing her resources. Still, she never complained and Rigoberto resolved to do something that would help her out in some way.

Once the groceries were put away, his grandmother sat wearily at the small table. She picked up the small stack of mail that Rigoberto had laid there not long before. Not much was there. The bare remnants of a Spartan life. Phone and utility bills, the occasional letter from her home town, but never any credit card offers or pleas from charities. Just the essentials for a life teetering on the edge of survival. She sighed, laying the stack down.

"*Mijo,* I'm tired. I lay down a few minutes, OK?" She wandered toward the back of the trailer and quietly closed the door to her small bedroom.

Rigoberto knew that his grandmother's age and life of hard work were catching up with her. He also knew that he could not continue living with her unless he found some way to make money. He was just sixteen, with a small frame and the smooth skin of a child. He was not yet large enough to be hired for construction or other heavy labor. He was only a fair student and did not think he could handle a job with a lot of numbers or writing. Perhaps he could work in a fast food place, just to bring in some money. He was thinking about what places might hire him when he heard the sound of tires crunching on the gravel outside their trailer. He peeked through the window blinds in the kitchen window and saw that a woman was getting out of her green sedan. It was dusty and a hubcap was missing on the front tire. He didn't recognize the woman, and her professional attire – cream-colored blouse over a dark grey skirt, black pumps and a large black tote case – indicated that she wasn't from this neighborhood. Most everyone in the complex wore work clothes for construction or landscaping jobs, or else uniforms to work in the service business. The woman studied a paper in her hand, glanced at the door, and approached. Rigoberto scurried to the back of the trailer, where his grandmother was resting on her double bed.

"Tata," he whispered, standing just above her, "there's someone here."

Rosa's eyes opened, and she sat up, her face searching his. "You stay here," she said, and left the room, closing the door behind her. Rigoberto stood there for a moment, his thoughts racing. Once he heard the door open and his grandmother's voice offer a quiet greeting, he decided to listen in as best he could. He sat next to the door, his ear resting on the rough, brown wood.

"Are you Rosa Saenz?" asked a woman's voice. Rigoberto heard her voice as clearly as if he were in the same room; the door was obviously made of thin materials.

"Yes," answered his grandmother.

"My name is Sarah Sanmiguel. I'm a social worker with the Department for the Protection of Children in Phoenix." She paused. "May I come in?"

Rigoberto imagined his grandmother making a quick glance at the bedroom door where he sat, and then motioning the woman inside. He heard the woman's steps on the metal stairs leading up to the door.

"Please have a seat," said his grandmother. He heard a scooting from one of the dining room chairs being pulled on the linoleum tile floor. There was a pause. "You want some water?" she asked.

"Oh, yes, that would be very nice. It's very hot out today."

The refrigerator door opened and closed, and Rigoberto heard water being poured into a glass.

Another pause, and he imagined that the woman was having a drink before she got into the reason for her visit. He heard the sound of the glass being set on the Formica table.

"Mrs. Saenz, I'm here on behalf of the DPC in Denver. I have some difficult news."

Rigoberto couldn't be sure, but it sounded as if his grandmother shifted in her chair. He could picture her sitting with her spine erect, hands on her knees, her face impassive. "Yes?" she said, her voice quivering only a little.

"There have been some, um, developments in your family." She cleared her throat. "Your daughter-in-law, Ginger, is in the hospital, your son Rodolfo is in jail, and your grandson Fernando is dead. You're the closest family that your grandson Manuel has. He's in protective custody right now, but we were wondering if you might be able to take him in until your daughter-in-law gets well. I realize that this is a lot to tell you right now." The chair squeaked as she shifted her weight. "Would you like some time to think about this?"

Rigoberto began rocking as he sat on the floor, his mind whirling. Had his father's drinking and anger finally come to this? He stifled a sob forming at the back of his throat. *Could I have prevented this somehow? Could I have saved my family?* He pictured his brother Nino's chubby face smiling at him when he would play with him. Rigoberto covered his mouth with his fist. *I'm so sorry, Nino, I'm so, so sorry.*

"Can you tell me what happened?" his grandmother asked.

"We're not entirely sure, but the police suspect it was a case of domestic violence. Your son was passed out drunk when they picked him up. They think he beat up your daughter-in-law pretty badly and shook the baby until it died. Manny found them both. He's pretty upset and scared, as you might imagine. He's with a foster family and will be until you decide if you can take him in." The social worker's voice made it sound so common, so factual, as if she were reading the weather report. Rigoberto wondered if it weren't something she had to say on a regular basis. Just another story. Just another sad statistic.

There was a long pause as his grandmother found her voice. "Yes, I take him, of course. He is family. Of course." Her voice sounded distant and very sad.

The women's voices continued as Rigoberto's attention turned inward. He could imagine his father coming home drunk again and beating his mother. He'd seen it many times. He hated his father for what he did to his mother and, later, to himself. As he grew, his anger at his father increased. During the last year, he would stand up to his father and tell him what he thought and that's when his father's fists would be aimed at him.

His father's fists never seemed to tire. Rather than exhausting their rage on Rigoberto, their anger would seem to grow before they turned again toward his mother. Rigoberto knew that he was not helping his mother, and living with his father was becoming impossible. That's why he finally left in April.

He remembered the last fight he'd had with his father. He remembered the curses, the anger, the cries to stop from his mother. He remembered trying to defend himself, but his father was too tall and too strong. Finally, he ended up wrapped into a small ball on the floor, crying and coughing up bile. He rocked himself while he heard the yelling and blows rain on his mother in the kitchen.

When Rigoberto's grandmother opened the door to her bedroom in the trailer, she found him, arms wrapped tight around his bent legs, sobbing and rocking himself on the floor.

CHAPTER 7

As the plane landed in Honolulu, Rissa peered out the window in gloom. It was raining in paradise. On one hand, she was happy to be away from her job for a while, and even happier that one of Carly's children came down with chickenpox so she had to stay home. On the other hand, Rissa wasn't too keen on being by herself for a whole week. She had packed her suitcase with an armful of books she had been meaning to read, but she also had hoped to work on her suntan.

She looked out the window again. The rain poured and Rissa saw the tall palm trees lean in the wind. *Do the Hawaiian islands get hurricanes?*, Rissa thought. *Just my luck.* As the passengers started to leave, she set herself up for a week's worth of heavy reading. *It will be like a mini-retreat*, she told herself.

Burly Bill and Breakfast Bob hadn't provided transportation to the Marquis Hotel, and the hotel didn't provide a shuttle from the airport, so Rissa's gloom deepened when she saw the taxi's final bill. She reminded herself to set aside some money for the ride back to the airport, and budget herself until then. *That's OK,* she thought, *I'm used to being frugal.*

The Marquis Hotel was not one of the newest in Honolulu. The rain only emphasized its box-like construction, with windows lined up in rows above each other and a few cracks defacing the plain white stucco façade. A couple of palm trees, in desperate need of trimming, swayed near the front driveway. Next to the hotel's entryway, a large white plastic planter, in faux Grecian style, held a couple of dying plants and an assortment of cigarette butts. As Rissa got out of the taxi, a burst of wind and rain slapped her in the face and she was instantly soaked. Her mood darkened.

Once in the room on the fourth floor, Rissa opened the heavy maroon curtains. The window presented her with a spectacular view of a parking lot. She sighed and looked around the room. Pretty basic, she thought. Bed, TV cabinet, a mini-fridge, bath, sink, toilet, one closet. Hung above the bed was a lone painting, which looked like a reproduction of an untalented child's impression of Hawaiian plant life. *Only in hotels do you see such ugly artwork,* she thought. She set the locks on the door and unpacked her things.

She placed her books in a row on the cabinet. *Wuthering Heights, The Alchemist,* a book on Buddhist meditation, and a couple of mystery novels. She even borrowed her neighbor's tattered copy of Michener's *Hawaii.* She looked over the titles to see which one appealed to her first. She scrunched her face and decided to dry off and change before sitting down to read. Her stomach rumbled. She needed to find a cheap place to eat.

Once changed and her hair blown dry by the whiny hairdryer attached to the bathroom wall, Rissa looked at the line of books again, blindly grabbed one and stuffed it into her satchel. She checked her wallet once more, did some mental figuring, and went downstairs.

The clerk at the front desk pointed the way to the hotel's only restaurant, which Rissa soon determined was both dreary and dirty. *I'd like to see the beach even if it is raining,* she thought. She borrowed the clerk's umbrella, promising that she'd return it before the clerk's shift ended, and went looking for some lunch.

She walked three blocks toward the beach, passing construction sites for new hotels, and four more blocks along the lineup of beachfront hotels to find one that looked nice but not too expensive. Many of the hotels posted their menus outside, which helped. Gusts of wind and rain sprayed Rissa in spite of her best efforts with the umbrella.

Hungry and wet, she settled on the Tiki Tiki Lounge and Karaoke Bar at the Blue Surf Hotel. It was a little early for lunch and only held a couple of other people. Rissa sat at a table near a window overlooking the ocean. She sighed. *It's beautiful even in the rain,* she thought.

She quickly scanned the menu, ordered a seafood salad and coffee, and after wiping the rain off her hands and arms, grabbed the book in her satchel and prepared to lose herself for a while. *Wuthering Heights.* She exhaled with satisfaction. *Perfect in this weather.*

A drop of rain slid from her scalp down her nose. She grabbed a napkin and patted her face and head. Unthinking, her fingers made a quick adjustment to her bangs, covering her birthmark. A baritone voice from the corner chuckled.

"Ooh, look at you. The drowning romantic."

Rissa whirled around, seeing a man grinning at her. Blond, tan, in a crisp linen shirt, khaki slacks, and expensive leather sandals, he had one long leg crossed over the other and bobbed his foot. His smile was casual and self-assured, his eyes mocking. Rissa stared, surprised someone would talk to her like that.

In less than a week, he would become her new best friend.

CHAPTER 8

Rissa was still mopping the rain off her head when the man sat, uninvited, at her table.

"I just love that book. I studied it when I was an English literature major at the University of Chicago."

Rissa stared.

"I should introduce myself. The name is Irving Waverly the third, professional student." He offered his hand.

After a moment's thought, Rissa shook his hand. "My name's Clarissa Wright, but most people call me Rissa." A shy smile sneaked across her lips.

"Look, I don't mean to seem forward or anything – believe me, I'm not that kind of guy – but I can tell you're not part of the B & B crowd any more than I am."

"B & B crowd?" Rissa asked.

"Beer and boobs. Either flashing them or groping them. I'm not interested in that sort of thing, and I can tell you're not, either." He grinned at her.

She stared again. "OK, Irving the third, what is a professional student?"

He laughed. "You can call me Trey. A professional student. Well, that's a bit of a story, but I guess you're entitled. After all, there's not much else to do on a day like today," he said, looking out the window, "and the person I was waiting for hasn't shown up, so we have time."

He leaned back in his chair. "I am the son and grandson of the heads of Waverly Industries, located in Boston. You've heard of it?"

Rissa shook her head and put down her wet napkin. She laid her book on the table as the waiter served her lunch and coffee. After taking a sip, she sat back to listen.

"Oh, go ahead and eat. It's fine," Trey said, waving his hands at her plate. "Waverly Industries is a multi-interest corporation, very profitable, very well-respected, and very boring." He chuckled. "My parents love the fact that they are high on the social standing list, and adore seeing their names on the society page. What they *don't* like is anything that might jeopardize their conservative sense of respectability. Like me." He pointed to himself and twisted his lips in amusement.

Rissa speared a shrimp and said, "Oh, I don't know. You don't seem that bad. Like you said, you're not part of the B & B crowd." She grinned.

"Oh, but you're wrong. Alas, I don't fit into their very narrow definition of how a son should be," Trey said, flipping his wrist in an exaggerated feminine pose and raising his eyebrows, "and so I spend their money hopping around the country from university to university and studying anything that might interest me. So here I am, twenty-nine years old, and a professional student at university number twelve."

"That's crazy. You mean that they can't accept you as you are? This *is* the twenty-first century, after all."

"Well, there are some people who value the opinion of someone else, whether it is their friends, their social class, or their church, more than the conviction of their own heart. That's sad, but that's the way it is."

"I'm sorry to hear that." Her eyes were shadowed in sympathy. "I work full-time as a human services aide, am studying part-time for my bachelor's in social work, and I've seen how parents can be horrible to their children. And it isn't always physical, either." She nodded in understanding.

Trey shrugged. "No boyfriend?"

Rissa's eyebrows shot up, but then she reconsidered. "No, no time. Not much energy, either." She gave him a lopsided smile.

Trey nodded. "Anyway, what brings you here? Vacation?"

"Yes, I won this seven-day, six-night trip here in a radio station contest. They obviously got a cut rate on the hotel. A friend from work was supposed to come with me, but her kid got sick and she had to defer her trip until later. So, I'm here with my books." She gestured to the novel on the table.

"You're going to get bored after the second day. Look, I'm on break between spring semester and summer term, so why don't I show you around a bit? I'm currently majoring in Hawaiian studies and know some interesting places. What do you say?"

Rissa considered. He was probably right about being bored very soon, especially if the weather prohibited her from working on her tan. She nodded. "OK, how about tomorrow?" she asked.

"Great. Give me a call when you're ready and I'll swing by your hotel. Let me give you my card." He took a card from his wallet and handed it to her.

She stared at it for a second. It was in heavy cream cardstock with gold script lettering. "You have to reprint your card every time you move to a new school, don't you?"

"Sure. What better way to remind my parents that I still exist than to keep sending them lots of bills?" He grinned. "I'll let you finish your lunch. See you tomorrow."

Rissa watched him leave and picked up her book. She stared out the window, wondering if she had made a mistake. Still, her instincts, which she relied on so much at her job, told her that he was safe. She'd think about it again tomorrow and determine if she really wanted to call or not, she decided. She put another bite of salad in her mouth and, chewing, started to read.

CHAPTER 9

"Hey, Rigo, wanna go out?" Rigoberto's friend Sammy, who was the only person in his new high school who seemed willing to get to know this quiet new student, was leaning out of the car window and yelling at the outline of Rigo's head in the trailer window. Rigoberto finished drying the dinner dishes and made his excuses to his grandmother, saying he'd be back later. He jumped into Sammy's ancient sedan, bleached a dull green by the desert sun, with portions of the paint eaten completely away. A short bungee cord held up the sagging rear fender and red plastic tape covered a broken taillight. Gravel shot from underneath the tires as Sammy gunned the engine to leave.

"Where are we going?" said Rigo. It really didn't matter. Just to get out of the cramped trailer was enough for him. *I don't want to think right now. I don't want to remember.* The sadness on his grandmother's face and the guilt that gnawed at his soul were more than he could bear. He rolled down the window, although he knew the night air wasn't enough to cool the rivers of sweat already forming on his back and thighs.

"I dunno. Where you wanna go?" asked Sammy. They drove around for a while, ogling a few girls brave enough to walk along the streets at that hour, and ended up ordering some soft drinks at a drive-through. As they sat in the car savoring the icy sodas, they saw a group of six boys talking and smoking cigarettes. Their low-slung jeans, brand-name sneakers, tee shirts covered with graphics of skulls or graffiti-style writing seemed to be a kind of street uniform in this neighborhood. Rigo didn't know the boys, but judged them to be tough types.

One of the boys from the group looked their way and waved at Sammy to come join them. Sammy got out of the car and Rigo followed him with reluctance.

"Yo, Sammy, what's up," said the boy, lifting his chin in a kind of greeting. He was a couple of years younger than the others, maybe sixteen or seventeen. Rigo, with his short stature and lean build, felt out of place.

"Not much, Omar. Hey, this is my friend Rigo." Sammy patted Rigo's shoulder; Rigo copied the raised-chin greeting.

The boys talked a bit, passing around cigarettes and bragging about girls they'd had and cars they'd raced. Rigo noticed that one of the group, a tall boy named Cesar with pockmarked skin and slicked-back hair, kept his dark eyes on Rigo, studying him. Finally, he spoke.

"Let's go somewhere else. I know a real quiet place, where we can do something more than suck on these lousy cigarettes," Cesar said as he flicked a smoking butt onto the pavement. "What do you say?" The group was quiet, watching Sammy and Rigo. Sammy laughed and said, sure, that was OK. Rigo could feel it was some sort of test. He met Cesar's steely gaze.

The group split up, some in Cesar's car and some in Sammy's, and drove west a few miles. They were getting into old farmland, at the edges of the suburbs, where patches of cotton and alfalfa still grew, and old farm shacks leaned precariously in the desert winds. After a while, Cesar's car stopped behind an abandoned farm house. Weathered boards covered the window openings and graffiti covered the walls. Tall weeds, dried out from lack of rain, swayed in the hot breeze. Cesar kicked the plywood that covered the back doorway and entered. He lit his lighter and found a couple of candles on apple crates, lighting them. The rest of the boys came in.

Before entering, Rigo pulled Sammy's arm. "Hey, let's not stay too long, huh?" he said. Sammy shrugged and smiled.

One of the boys had already pulled out a bottle of cheap vodka and was passing it around. Rigo looked around the room in the murky light. He saw more graffiti on the walls, with large balloon letters proclaiming the tag names of various people who had visited this place before. Empty bottles, beer and cheap liquor, littered the floor, and the boys either sat on the floor or on one of the few apple crates that could be found. An old table stood at the edge of the room, its wooden surface littered with drug paraphernalia and its surface grooved with the initials of past visitors. Pigeons grunted in the attic and the air stank of cigarettes, beer, and sweat. He could hear the distant highway to Los Angeles from the cracks between the boards on the windows, but saw no lights from passing cars.

As the liquor took effect, the boys grew louder and started hitting each other in mock fights. They recounted past exploits, trying to prove who was the bravest. Rigo sat and listened, still aware of Cesar's eyes trained on him.

After a time, Cesar stood up and dragged the table to the center of the room. He pushed a couple of the boys off their apple crates and placed them on opposite sides of the table.

"So, you think you guys have *cajones*? I know how you can prove it." He took out a switchblade, flicked it open, and stabbed it into the table. The boys stood. A few laughed in recognition of the game.

"Here's how it goes," continued Cesar. He put his left hand in the center of the table and, grabbing a piece of chalk from his pocket, traced around his hand onto the surface of the table. "You put your hand here," Cesar motioned to the outline of the hand on the table. "And I stand here and drop the knife from up here," he stretched his arm high over his head with the knife in his hand, dangling between his thumb and index finger. "Then I let go," he said, releasing the knife to drop into the table. The blade landed, quivering, between two of the fingers drawn on the table. The boys roared with laughter. "You stay, you win. You flinch, you lose," said Cesar, his inky eyes staring into Rigo's.

Sammy had drunk too much too fast, and was tripping over himself in his laughter. The boys grabbed him and sat him on the apple crate, placing his hand inside the chalk outline. Sammy was still laughing as Cesar slowly lifted his hand high into the air, the knifepoint swaying between his two fingers. As Sammy looked at the knife, his laughter ceased. He swallowed and beads of sweat popped up on his forehead. Cesar's eyes traveled between the knife and Sammy, and a tight smile pulled on his lips. Sammy licked his lips.

The blade fell, but Sammy's hand was already halfway off the table. As soon as the knife hit a mark inside the handprint on the table, the boys grabbed Sammy and pushed him off the apple crate, pummeling him with their fists and kicking him in the stomach. The smell of vomit filled the room and the boys left Sammy moaning and gagging on the floor. "You flinch, you lose," Cesar said, lighting a cigarette and taking a long, slow drag.

Rigo felt himself being lifted up onto the apple crate. A hand grabbed his arm, but he jerked it away. He placed his hand inside the chalk drawing himself, and stared at Cesar with defiance. "Oh, somebody with *cajones*, eh?" said Cesar, laughing softly.

Cesar's arm rose more slowly than before, the knife's edge glinting in the light of Cesar's cigarette. Rigo slowed his breathing, training his eyes on Cesar's and forcing his insides into steel, as he'd learned to do from years of his father's abuse. He could hear Cesar's breathing quicken.

The knife fell. It landed with a thud into the table between Rigo's second and third fingers. He did not allow himself to blink, but returned Cesar's stare. After the knife stopped shaking, he pulled it out of the table and gave it to Cesar. Then he pulled his hand off the table.

"OK, so you have one *cajón*. Do you have two?" The two boys, one six inches taller than the other, stood, their eyes locked in a silent battle of wills. After a few seconds, Rigo sat down on the apple crate and placed his hand back on the table. The boys around them roared and passed around the bottle again.

The knife dangled high above the table. Cesar's eyes bore into Rigo's and Rigo once more slowed his breathing and willed his guts into iron. Sammy was recovered enough to sit up and watch. He drew a shaky arm across his mouth and chin to wipe off the remaining vomit.

Cesar's fingers parted. The knife flew down. Rigo, from a place deep inside himself, watched its flight as if in slow motion. He did not stir or blink, or even let himself feel anything but a steely distance. All he was aware of was the knife, its movement, and Cesar's eyes.

The knife landed, with a sickening thud, in the middle of Rigo's hand. It had missed the bones and pinned the flesh of his palm to the table. The boys were silent. Cesar stared, his tight smile gone. He took a step back.

Rigo slowly arose and grabbed the knife handle. In one swift motion, he pulled it out of his hand. With drops of blood clinging to its point, he waved it in a slow arc before him as if to cut the line of eye contact between himself and Cesar. He wiped the blade on his jeans, clicked it closed and slipped it into his right front pocket. Putting his injured hand into his left front pocket, he offered his other hand to Sammy to help him stand. "Let's go, Sammy," he murmured.

CHAPTER 10

Sammy's car bumped down the dirt road as it sped away from the abandoned house. Rigo exhaled deeply and allowed the steel in his gut to loosen. His jeans pocket was soaked with blood and waves of nausea flowed over him. A whiff of the vomit still on Sammy's shirt made his stomach lurch.

"Hey, slow down, will ya?" said Rigo. He needed something to staunch the blood oozing from his hand. He looked around the car. There was a uniform shirt from Sammy's job as a hamburger flipper on the back seat. Rigo grabbed it and gingerly pulled his hand from his pocket. He was glad the knife blade had missed the bones. He gently flexed his fingers and did not think any tendons were cut, either. He wrapped his hand in the uniform shirt.

Sammy, back on paved road and urging the car faster, glanced at Rigo's hand. "Hey, that's my Mr. Burger shirt! They're gonna make me pay for it!"

Rigo gave him a sidelong glance. "Asshole. It was *your* friends who did this, so it seems only right." He pulled the shirt tighter around his hand and tucked one end under the bandage to hold it there. The hand was starting to throb and the after-effects of the adrenaline rush made him feel light-headed and weak. He needed some water and something to eat, soon.

Sammy's mouth tightened. "I only knew J.B., the younger one. The others I'd seen around, but they weren't my friends." A note of indignation crept into his voice. "Besides, you weren't the only one hurt, you know."

"Yeah, well you've lived here longer than I have and you should know what these guys are like. Bad news, every one of 'em. I'm beginning to think you're bad news, too." Rigo spit the words out like venom. His head pounded and he was trying to keep from vomiting.

They drove in tense silence for a couple of miles when they emerged from the farming areas and re-entered the edges of town. Rigo spotted a gas station with a quick mart inside. "Hey, stop here. I gotta get something to eat."

Sammy swerved off the road and did not break until they were in front of the quick mart. The car jerked to a stop so hard that Rigo had to put his hand on the dashboard to keep from hitting his head. "What a loser," he said under his breath.

Sammy motioned to the quick mart. "Waddya want?" he demanded.

"What are you talking about? I'll get it myself," Rigo snapped.

"Like hell you will. Look at you. You're covered in blood and look like you're going to hold up the place. They'll set off the alarm the minute you step in there." He held out his hand for some money. "So, waddya want?"

Rigo searched his back pocket for a couple of bills. He slapped them into Sammy's hand. "Get me some crackers and a soda, like 7-Up or something."

Sammy left the car, slamming the door so that the car rocked. Rigo leaned back in the seat, propping his right hand on the car door to shield his eyes. With no warning, his stomach lurched and he leaned forward and vomited between his legs onto the floor of the car. The stench filled the car.

Sammy returned and started to swear as he saw what had happened. "You asshole! This is my brother's car! You messed it up and it's gonna stink for weeks!" Sammy was livid, both angry at his friend and afraid of his brother's fists. "You call me a loser, well, you're the loser for showing off to those guys! You're the one that got yourself hurt!" Sammy's breath was quick and shallow as his voice became a shout. "Get out! Just get out! Take your food and just get out!" Sammy threw the box of crackers and the can of soda at Rigo, who carefully avoided stepping in the pool on the car's floor as he stepped outside.

"Hey, Sammy, you're not gonna just leave me here, are ya?"

Sammy was still yelling curses at him as his car sped off. Rigo watched the car fishtail onto the road and followed its path until it became two red dots far in the distance. He slumped and sat on the curb by the quick mart, out of sight of the cashier.

He took a sip of the soda and his stomach settled almost immediately. After a few more sips, he ate some crackers and the pounding in his head subsided. He inhaled deeply and looked at himself in the yellow glare of the florescent lights. His jeans were smeared in blood, with a large stain around his left pocket. More drops decorated his grey tee-shirt, whether from blood or vomit, he could only guess.

He thought for a few minutes. He couldn't go into the quick mart because of how he looked. He had only a couple of dollars and he didn't think the bus ran that late at night. He didn't want to call his grandmother because he really didn't know where he was. How many miles was he from home? Ten, fifteen? Perhaps he could start walking and later try to hitch a ride. Still, his appearance wouldn't help him. As he continued to think, he ate more crackers to build his strength.

He watched as a blue Chevy sedan pulled in to get gas. A man in a navy blue suit and well-worn leather shoes got out of the car to pay the cashier before filling up. Rigo made himself small and the man did not look his way as he entered the quick mart.

Being without many options reminded Rigo of that pinched feeling he had right before he left Denver, when he realized that he didn't have enough money to buy the bus ticket to Phoenix. After borrowing from some of his friends and combining that with his meager savings, he realized that he was still short on cash. The night before he left, he took some money from his father's wallet while the man lay snoring after a long evening of drinking. Rigo had felt bad that he was taking money from his brothers and mother, but assured himself that he would find some way to help them some day. *Sometimes you gotta do what you gotta do*, he thought.

He took one last gulp from the soda can and, crouching low, ran to the far side of the car. He tested the rear door handle to see if the alarm would sound. It didn't. Keeping low, he opened the door and slid in, closing the door as quietly as he could. Next, he got on the floor and folded his body into a small ball.

He heard the man's shoes make soft slapping sounds on the cement and the man whistle as he filled the tank with gas. After a couple of minutes, the pump shut off and the man put back the gas cap and returned the nozzle to the pump. Rigo's throat grew dry as the man opened the car door and sat behind the wheel.

The car started to go toward the road and Rigo counted to five so as to be out of the view of the cashier at the quick mart.

With one quick motion, he unfolded his body and opened the switchblade. He put its stained point at the side of the man's neck. The man winced on instinct, and the point drew a bead of blood. Rigo said in a husky voice, "Do what I tell ya, and you won't get hurt."

CHAPTER 11

Trey was right. Spending the whole afternoon reading was getting to be boring. The rain wasn't letting up, and Rissa ached to see some sights. After a light dinner, she did a quick computer search on Irving Waverly III. After satisfying herself that he wasn't a convicted serial killer but indeed someone with frequent address changes to university towns, she decided to call him. They made an appointment to meet the next morning.

The following day, Rissa pressed her face against the window of her room. If she scooted herself to the far left corner and stood on tiptoe, she could see a sliver of blue between buildings. *At least I'll be able to say I had an ocean view room*, she thought. The sky was still heavy with clouds, but no rain yet.

Promptly at 9:00, she went downstairs to find Trey sitting in his metallic blue BMW with the top down. She prayed the sky would withhold its rain at least until they reached the museum. Her neck strained with the sudden acceleration of the car, accustomed to the slower tempo of her ancient Civic. Rissa held onto the door, her feet firmly planted on the invisible brake pedal on the passenger floorboard, as Trey weaved between gawking tourists' cars and slow buses. All the while, with his right hand illustrating his ideas in the air, he praised the wonders of the famous Bishop Museum.

The museum is indeed wonderful, thought Rissa, although she noticed it took a full ten minutes for her knees to stop shaking from the drive there. They spent most of their time in the Polynesian Hall, where Trey explained the uses and meanings of some of the more unusual religious objects like the totems and tiki carvings, and in the Kahili Room where portraits of the various monarchs and their feather standards were displayed. She felt sadness and remorse in the way her own country's government had overthrown this vital and proud leadership.

Rissa and Trey decided to take a quick coffee break and sit for a while. Their feet were tired after a couple hours of doing the museum shuffle on the hard floors. Rissa was keen also in finding out why this tall, blond Easterner was so interested in the religion and culture of Pacific islanders.

Trey leaned back in his chair, one leg crossed over the other and foot bouncing, and asked, "So, why did you decide to become a human services aide?"

Rissa laughed. "You know, I wanted to find out more about you, too. You're really knowledgeable about this Hawaiian cultural stuff, and it strikes me as an odd fit."

Trey grinned. "I asked you first. Then, I'll tell you my story, at least the part about why I'm here."

"OK," answered Rissa. "Do you want the long version, or the 4-second sound bite?"

"The long version. We've got time."

"All right. It all started when I was nine and a couple of pigeons built a nest under the eaves outside my bedroom window."

"Pigeons got you into social work?"

"You wanted the long version," said Rissa with a smile. "Let me finish. Anyway, the pigeons built the nest and I watched as the mother bird sat on the eggs for days on end. I didn't think they'd ever hatch. After some time, though, they did and both the mother and father bird took turns feeding the chicks and the mother bird kept them warm at night until they got too big to sit on." Rissa sighed. "That's when I saw the ugly side of pigeon behavior."

"Besides the obvious messy stuff, right?"

"Well, that, too. But what happened was that one day there was a big wind storm and I came home from school and found the two babies – I had named them Peter and Patsy – on the ground. The feathers had grown in by then, but they were still a couple of weeks away from flying. Still, they had odd little wounds on their heads and Peter was nearly bald. I thought that they had scratched their heads in the fall, so I put on my gardening gloves, put them in a bucket, climbed the tree next to the house, and put them back in their nest."

"Did the mother bird accept them?" asked Trey.

"Yes, she was feeding them the next morning. But the next day I found them on the ground again, and poor Patsy had a big bloody gash in the top of her head. I put them back and, wouldn't you know, the same thing happened the following day."

"You couldn't blame the weather for all three days, could you?"

"No, it was windy only the first day. Well, by that time, the poor chicks were really banged up and Peter had some bloody wounds on his wing, too. So, I called the local vet, who told me to call the Game and Fish department, who referred me to a wildlife rescue group. My dad nearly had a fit about having to drive to this place 15 miles away in order to save some dirty little pigeons."

"Well, I'm sure you were convincing."

"I suppose so. The lady at the rescue center said that sometimes the father bird will try to kill the chicks in order to make the mother produce again, and to make sure that they were really his offspring. I had remembered seeing the father with the babies and hearing all sorts of noise, but I just thought he was feeding them. I didn't know he was trying to kill them."

"I'm surprised you didn't become a veterinarian."

"The fact of the matter is that I don't even like birds that much. Still, they were injured innocents in a bad situation, and I felt like they were my responsibility. I guess the feeling of responsibility just generalized from the creatures around my house to the powerless ones in society. And so I'm two years away from my degree in social work, and wondering if I can make a difference." Rissa pursed her lips, thinking of the toddler whom she had seen sleeping in his mother's arms just days before, and now lying cold and still in a Denver morgue.

Trey put his hand on her arm, seeing the sudden change in her demeanor. "Maybe you can't change the whole world, but you can brighten your corner of it. Just think of the generations of pigeons who have you to thank." They both laughed.

"OK, I've told my story," said Rissa, rubbing her neck. "Your turn. You really impressed me with all your knowledge about the artifacts in the museum. Why do you keep moving from school to school? Why not specialize in something, write books, teach, and become famous in your field?"

"You want the short version or the long version?" asked Trey with a bemused look.

Rissa's eyes twinkled in amusement. "The long version. We've got time." She leaned back and took another sip of coffee.

Trey sighed. "Did you know that aspen trees, which grow in your Rocky Mountains, appear to be separate trees but are in reality one huge organism?"

Rissa nodded with puzzlement. "Yes, I'd heard that."

Trey nodded. "Well, I've noticed through my studies that even though some things appear to be completely separate, they often share the same roots of underlying meaning. You see similar mythic stories which appear in far flung cultures, you see similar adaptive changes in creatures which don't have contact with each other, you see ideas or concepts," Trey searched for the words, "perhaps from widely different fields, which all point to some basic truth." Trey paused. "That's what I'm studying. I want to find that underlying truth. I want to develop a theory of ultimate reality."

"A theory of everything?"

"Well, maybe not everything, but the core truths which illuminate our everyday existence. That's what I want."

Rissa blew out air in a silent whistle. "That's huge. You may become famous yet. They'll have to call it the Trey Waverly Theory. That's got a nice ring to it."

Trey laughed. "Well, there are a lot more schools I haven't attended yet, and my parents seem willing to foot the bill until I'm old and grey." He shrugged. "There are worse things to dedicate one's life to."

"Like pigeons?"

"No," answered Trey with seriousness, "like a life without meaning."

CHAPTER 12

Not eager to climb back into Trey's speedy car yet, Rissa asked if they could revisit the Bishop Museum's gift shop. They entered the shop, shouldering their way around tourists eying the tee-shirts and shell necklaces.

"I want to find a little tiki god to put on my desk at work. Maybe it'll keep away bad luck and chatty co-workers."

Trey laughed. "You mean an 'aumakua figure?"

"Is that what you called those fierce-looking wooden god things with the human hair and shell eyes?" A gawky teenage boy shuffled between them, his eyes fixed on a poster high on the wall behind them. Rissa huffed and moved out of his way.

"Yes, there were a few of those in the museum. You can buy cheap replicas at any tourist shop. Anyway, it wouldn't keep away bad luck unless you understood the magic behind it."

"OK, explain." Rissa crossed her arms and braced herself for a lengthy lecture on Hawaiian deities.

"Well, the figure is just a representation of a personal god, not the god itself. Having one without understanding it would be as meaningful as a Buddhist praying to a St. Joseph figurine."

"So I need to understand the personal god part?" Rissa found the lights in the shop hot and felt her temper growing short.

A large woman in a crimson muu-muu bumped into Trey, momentarily knocking him off balance. He drew in a sharp breath and grabbed Rissa by the elbow. "Let's step outside for a moment, shall we?"

They stood under the stone porticos and enjoyed the cool, fresh air. Rissa noticed that the light breeze carried the scents of rain and fresh tropical flowers. Its sweetness calmed her.

Trey brushed off his trousers and continued. "In the mystical teachings of the Hawaiians, called Huna, every person is made of three parts. The lower animal self, which was just now activated when I almost snapped at that clumsy tourist, the middle self, which is talking to you now, and the higher selves."

"You say 'selves'? There's more than one?"

"One of the secret teachings that I've read is that each person has a pair of higher selves, really two in one, a male and female couple who are joined. Like twin brother and sister guardian angels."

"Two for the price of one. I like that."

"The thing is, the Hawaiians considered God too big of a concept for humans to fathom, so the closest things they had were their nature gods and their personal gods. So, they generally prayed to their personal gods and expected them to get whatever help they needed from the higher deities."

"You mean that the personal gods were like mediators between the individual human and the gods higher up on the ladder?"

Trey nodded. "Not only that, but the personal gods understood humans the best because they were once human themselves."

"You mean they got promoted? Is that like attaining enlightenment or something?"

Trey looked thoughtful. "I think it's a lot like some of the Buddhist teachings. From what I've studied, the middle self eventually goes through enough reincarnations that it attains a state of enlightenment and then moves up to become a higher self, and the lower self moves up to become a middle self."

"So what you're saying is that we were once lower animal selves and became middle selves when our higher selves were promoted, right?"

Trey nodded. "What I've been wondering lately, in formulating my Theory of Everything," his eyes twinkled, "is if the male-female higher selves are like the copulating gods that the soul meets, as described in the Tibetan Book of the Dead."

"Oh, I saw a TV program on that book once – there seemed to have been a whole lot of gods in sexual union in the afterlife. Deities in orgies! I love it!" she added, laughing and rubbing the back of her neck.

Trey's laughter turned serious. "Why do you keep massaging your neck?"

"Oh, it's so silly. I feel like I've been bitten or something, but I looked in the mirror this morning and didn't see anything."

Trey grabbed her shoulders and turned her around. "May I look?" He moved her ponytail out of the way as she pointed to the area that was bothering her.

"Nope, nothing."

Rissa smiled. "Maybe somebody's personal god is attacking me – what do you think?" She playfully slapped his arm as they walked back to his car.

"Or maybe it's your higher self reminding you that it's time for lunch."

CHAPTER 13

"Keep driving," Rigo growled. He pushed the point of the switchblade deeper into the man's neck. The drop of blood became a thin sliver of red flowing down the man's neck.

"Hey, take it easy," the man said, straining to control his voice. "I can help you."

"Shut up," snapped Rigo. Inside his head, thoughts swirled: *What do I do now? Where are we going to go? What am I going to do with this guy?* "Keep driving and turn when I tell ya."

Rigo's eyes, adjusted to the dark, scanned the inside of the car. On the back seat next to him lay a brown briefcase. The opening edge underneath the handle bore the initials, D.E. Glancing at the road and keeping his right hand steady holding the knife, Rigo used his injured left hand to move the briefcase into position so he could open it. For a moment, his fingertips caressed the soft leather. *Like my baby brother's skin*, he thought. The thought doused him with sadness. His baby brother was dead.

Rigo forced himself to put the thought into the back of his mind. *Focus.* He opened the briefcase. Inside were papers in file folders. He couldn't make out the writing on the tabs for the file folder, but a passing car illuminated a letter on top of the stack. "David Ezker, Mayor, Henderson, Arizona," read the heading. The lights from the passing car faded before Rigo could read more.

"Hey, you a mayor?" Rigo asked the man.

"Um, yes, I am. If you let me, I could help you out," the man paused to study the face of the boy in the rearview mirror. "Are you in trouble? I know people who could be of assistance."

Rigo studied David Ezker's face in the mirror. Short, dark brown hair, a wide brow beaded with perspiration, a pair of intelligent eyes framed by laugh lines, a prominent nose, and full lips. Dark stubble grew over the lower half of his face. He looked like he'd had a long day.

For an instant, their eyes met in the rearview mirror. Rigo jerked back as if he'd been slapped. The force of the gaze momentarily confused him. What had he seen in those blue-grey eyes? Intelligence, directness, a powerful sense of self, and – what could he call it? – the feeling that he was both seen and cared about. Rigo, in his sixteen years on Earth, had never encountered compassion before. It took a full minute before Rigo's anger and confusion reappeared.

He put the knife tip back at the man's neck. "Keep driving," he whispered.

They drove for over half an hour, with Rigo occasionally giving directions to turn right or left, until both felt they were completely lost. They were far from the city by now, driving in the desert west of Phoenix, past Buckeye, past Wintersburg and Tonopah, and now heading toward hilly desert country. Rigo was eager to get off the highway in case the car was spotted. He saw a dirt road leading off to the right and told the man to take it. The car jumped and jerked with the rocks and holes in the road. Rigo kept the knife at the man's neck while his eyes searched for somewhere to stop and hide. His mind was formulating a plan.

In the glow of the car's headlights, Rigo saw a smaller road, choked with weeds, off to the left. He told the man to take it. The car slowed to a crawl as the man negotiated the rocks and tumbleweeds that dotted the road. In the distance, Rigo could see the outline of a dwelling. As they drew near it, he saw it was abandoned. The shack leaned on its foundation as if it had lived through too many windstorms. The windows had long since broken, and whoever patched boards over the holes had left long ago. The boards were old and rotting, and one sagged as if its nails had loosened in a couple of corners. Rigo noticed that the building was free of graffiti and trash. The gangs and drug dealers hadn't discovered it yet.

A small hill separated the building from the highway; the sounds of passing traffic were far in the distance. *We'll be safe from spying eyes for the night*, Rigo thought.

Rigo ordered the man to park the car between the hill and the building. They stopped and sat for a minute in the dark.

The man cleared his throat. "Hey, if you need some light, I have a flashlight in my glove compartment. I'd rather not step on anything that could bite or sting me."

Rigo nodded. "OK, but do it slow. Don't do anything stupid." He gave the knife a slight jab in the man's neck. The man took in a sharp breath, steadied himself, and slowly removed the flashlight from the glove compartment. He started to hand it to Rigo, who said, "No, you take it. Let's get out."

The man switched on the flashlight as they both moved out of the car. Rigo kept the knife at the man's neck as they moved toward the old building.

The step leading up to the small porch was broken, so the man took a large step onto the porch itself. The boards creaked and sagged under his weight, but held. Behind him, Rigo had picked up something and then bounded onto the porch. He put the knife back at the man's neck, urging him into the building.

The door was ajar, held onto its frame by one rusting hinge. The man shined the flashlight inside the building, checking for rattlesnakes and scorpions, and half expected to find the bones of an old rancher. It smelled of dust and decay, not death. The yellow light revealed nothing more than dirt and dried vegetation that had blown in through the open door. The man took a step inside and, as he did so, crumpled like a puppet whose strings had just been cut, falling and rolling onto his side.

Rigo stood over him, rock in hand. "Nighty-night," he said.

CHAPTER 14

Rigo took the man's tie off and used it to bind his hands and feet together behind him. *He won't go far now*, he thought.

He took the flashlight and went back to the car. He pulled out the briefcase and took the keys from the ignition. He opened the trunk and found a couple of gallon-sized plastic containers of water, three paper bags from a local grocery store, one bungee cord with a hook on each end used to tie down loads, and a steering wheel club.

Using his good hand, Rigo made several trips to carry the briefcase, water and cord back to the building. The man was still and quiet, but breathing. Rigo thought for a moment and grabbed the keys and went outside again.

He started the car and pulled it under an old ironwood tree. Its branches were more skeletal than leafy in the moon's glow, but its ancient bows would provide at least some cover for the car in case someone were to fly over the site. Before he shut off the car, he saw that just beyond the tree was a sharp drop-off into a wash. *It must have been a river many years ago, before everything got dammed up,* thought Rigo. The old tree was surviving on whatever moisture the wash gathered from passing storms. *Be strong and survive, just like that old tree,* Rigo told himself. He spent a minute thinking of his nine-year-old brother who would be coming to live with them soon. He needed to be the man of the family now.

Rigo turned on the dome light and searched the glove compartment. David Ezker's insurance and registration cards were in there; Rigo pocketed them. Also, a tire gauge, a small first-aid kit, and a fist-sized object in a leather pouch.

Rigo pulled out the pouch. It was heavy. He opened the snap and felt inside. It was cold and metal. He pulled it out. A small gun.

Perfect, he thought.

He put the gun back into its case and took the first-aid kit. His left hand, now that the adrenaline rush was abating, was throbbing again. He exited the car, shut the door, and returned to the building.

The man was moving a bit and moaning, so Rigo used the cord he'd found in the trunk to retie the man's hands and feet behind him. He took off the man's shoes and socks and stuffed one of the socks into the man's mouth.

Good, now I can think.

He opened one of the plastic containers of water and took a swig. He grimaced at the sour taste, but swallowed anyway. It had been in the heat too long.

He sat on the floor, opened the briefcase and aimed the flashlight at its contents. A cell phone, several file folders of papers, a pen, two yellow mechanical pencils, and a notepad with the inscription, "From the desk of David Ezker, mayor." *Cute,* he thought.

Rigo randomly opened some of the files, but his eyes and mind couldn't focus on the meaning of the words on the pages. *Whew, I'm tired.*

He put his back against the wall next to the doorway, stretching his legs in front of him, and put the gun on top of its pouch next to his right hand. Closing his eyes, Rigo's mind reviewed what his next steps would be. It had become clear what he had to do.

With a sigh, he drifted off to sleep.

CHAPTER 15

Rissa felt small, sitting on an old wooden chair. She looked around, seeing that there were no other students in the classroom. Her feet almost touched the floor as she wiggled, trying to keep from slipping from her seat.

"Sit up and pay attention!" Rissa jumped as the teacher, a woman with grey hair pulled in a tight bun and wearing an old-fashioned flower print dress, rapped her pointer on her desk at the front of the room. She erased the words and figures on the dusty chalkboard and picked up a large piece of chalk.

"Write this down." The teacher pointed to the paper and large pencil on Rissa's desk. The old woman moved the chalk with exaggerated motions, speaking each symbol as she wrote:

"1 + 1 = 1"

The teacher whirled around to check that Rissa had recorded it on her paper. The pencil felt awkward in Rissa's hand, as if it were four sizes too big for her to hold. The numbers on her paper looked as if a small child had written them.

The teacher pointed to the board again and said, "Say it with me: One plus one equals one." Her voice was softer now, as if she were intoning a magic formula. "Repeat. One plus one equals one." Her voice was fading to a whisper. "Again. One plus one equals one." The woman became a shadow, with only the equation visible on the board. "Once more. One plus one equals one."

Rissa woke with a start and looked at blue numbers on the digital clock on the bed stand next to her. It read, 1:11.

CHAPTER 16

David Ezker awoke feeling groggy and dehydrated. His head pounded and his face felt like it was covered in grit. He couldn't move his arms or legs, and he was lying on an uneven, dirty floor. Something was stuffed in his mouth, making his thirst greater. He tried to think. *Where am I? Why can't I move?*

About ten feet away, a young man was sleeping, leaning against a wall. By the moonlight streaming through the open door, he could see the youth's profile. Not a large kid, David thought, with short legs and wiry build. His left hand lay on his lap and was wrapped in some sort of cloth and his right hand rested next to a small metallic object. David blinked his eyes. *What was that?* Suddenly, he remembered.

Damn, he thought, *the boy found the gun.*

The events of the last couple of hours tumbled back into his memory. He blinked, trying to get some of the dirt away from his eyes. He stared at the gun again, thinking his fears about it had been realized. His mind led him back to when he first received it, as a gift.

His best friend and city manager, Paul Salas, had first brought it up.

"David, you've got to carry some sort of protection, you know? You go around at all hours, often alone, and people talk to you. They want to see you whenever they're unhappy about something, sober or not, day or night, and sometimes they're mad. Not mad at you, but mad at the world. And one day, you're going to be their target because you're so damned *convenient*." Paul spat out the last word with a hint of anger.

"It comes with the job," David said, patting Paul on the shoulder. "That's why they elected me their mayor. Not because I'm so smart or anything, but because they know I'll listen. That's my job, really, to listen and let them know I'll do something if it's in my power to do it."

Paul frowned. "They should have elected you city shrink, if that's all there is to it." He folded his arms across his wide stomach. "Listen, just take the gun and keep it somewhere safe, just in case. You know, maybe in your briefcase, or somewhere in your car. I've already started the paperwork for carrying a concealed weapon. Just tell me you'll do it." His bushy eyebrows contorted in concern.

"You know, Paul, I just have a bad feeling about guns. I feel like they carry the energy of violence with them, and if I put that energy out there, it'll come right back at me. I know it sounds silly, but . . ." David shrugged, knowing his friend wouldn't understand.

"You and your energy stuff. Listen, if the bad energy comes back, send it my way because I was the one who first gave you the gun, OK?" He slapped David's left upper arm and laughed.

David nodded, knowing he wouldn't win this fight. He'd known Paul nearly all his life – they both grew up in the same town they now served. He knew that when Paul made his mind up about something, it was useless to argue. Over the next few weeks, he completed the requirements for carrying a concealed weapon, put the gun in his car's glove compartment, and forgot about it.

Until now. There it lay, shiny in the night's glow, next to a youth who was full of violence and anger. He'd seen it in the boy's eyes when he stole a glance in the rearview mirror earlier that evening. But he'd seen that look before, in the people he'd met over the years. It was a look born from powerlessness and frustration, whether from abuse, neglect, economic hardship, addiction, or any number of other things. That's what he fought to erase in the young people of his little town of 4500 souls. That's why he ran for mayor in the first place. He wanted to make a difference.

How could he make a difference here? *What did this kid plan to do?* His mind whirled with all the possibilities until he told himself that fear would not help the situation. He slowed his breaths, counting each one, until his mind quieted. *Pain is in the resistance*, he reminded himself. He rocked his head to find a more comfortable position, and continued counting his breaths until he drifted off to sleep.

CHAPTER 17

The next morning, Rissa woke up with a groan. Not only did the memory of the strange dream plague her, but her shoulder and leg muscles felt cramped and sore. *On top of that,* she grumbled to herself, *I've got a huge headache.*

After yesterday's trip to the Bishop Museum and lunch with Trey, she had returned to the hotel to sit on the beach under drifting clouds and read her book. She hoped the sporadic sunshine would help her tan. All in all, it had been a fun, relaxing day.

So, why do I feel so lousy? thought Rissa. Perhaps her body was just not used to feeling relaxed, without the pressure of responsibility. *Maybe that's it,* she reasoned.

She took a warm shower, ate breakfast, and gulped down a couple of aspirin when neither activity put a dent in her headache and soreness. After a while, she felt a little better and anticipated Trey's coming to pick her up for the day's trip.

Trey had been eager to show Rissa the campus of the University of Hawaii at Manoa. He had gushed, hands dancing as if to portray the forms he was describing, about the beautiful sculptures and the lovely and fragrant gardens on campus.

"They don't have such a wide variety of tropical ornamentals on other campuses," he had told her.

"Perhaps you should be a botany major," she teased.

Lips pursed, he raised his eyebrows. "That sounds like it could be interesting."

It was a warm, clear day, with the rain clouds long since blown away. Rissa figured she could work on her tan while riding in Trey's convertible.

Rissa learned that the key to staying calm while riding in Trey's car was to close her eyes at judicious moments. After the car jerked to a stop in the University parking lot, she opened her eyes to find Trey studying her.

"You seem a little distant today. Are you OK?" he asked.

"Oh, it's silly. I had a strange dream last night that's been bothering me," she said, not wanting to mention his Indy 500-style driving.

"Ooh, dreams!" he said as he laid a light hand on her shoulder, "I studied Jungian psychology at Texas A & M. Tell me all about it." He angled his body to face her and crossed his hands in his lap.

"Oh, we can walk and talk, can't we?" She was eager to leave the mobile death trap.

"Sure," said Trey, alighting from the car. He pointed to a direction that they should head toward.

The campus *was* lovely, just as he said. Her eyes feasted on the kaleidoscope of vivid colors of the Chinese violet, the powder-puff bush, hibiscus, irises and day lilies. Their flowers perfumed the air. She recognized a few of the trees – date and fan palms, citrus trees and magnolias – but Trey identified for her the mango, the Hawaiian candlenut tree, the sausage tree, and the dead-rat tree, so named because of its hairy brown fruit dangling from its branches. In between admiring the unusual flowers and trees, Rissa told him about her dream.

Trey considered for a minute and said, "Hmm. It sounds like those numbers have meaning. Tell me, what does the number one mean to you?"

Rissa paused, looking down in thought.

"No, don't think, just tell me" Trey instructed.

Her face grew serious. "One means . . . unity, wholeness. Being complete, I guess."

"And you said the teacher made you say the equation 1 + 1 = 1 how many times?"

"Four," answered Rissa.

"All right, what does the number four mean to you?"

She didn't let herself think too long. "Well, there are four directions, so I guess it means completely everything, maybe the Universe."

"So, your dream means . . ." he paused, choosing his words with care, "that a whole plus a whole equals a whole, and that in this unity the Universe is completed?"

"I guess so. Now, tell me what *that* means."

Trey waved off her question. "Now, tell me what time the clock said when you woke up?"

"It said 1:11. One-one-one."

Trey laughed and clapped his hands. "I love it! A perfect example of synchronicity." Seeing Rissa's puzzled expression, he continued, "Jung taught that when two or more things happen by coincidence in a way that has meaning to a person, that is synchronicity. He also taught that these events suggest that there is a governing dynamic that underlies the human experience."

"Translate, Professor." Rissa frowned and crossed her arms.

"It means the Universe is trying to tell you something."

CHAPTER 18

Rigo woke up with a start. Sunlight poured through the doorway and the cracks between the boards. In the light, he could see the building better. It was little more than a shack and the heat from too many summers had warped the boards so much that some of the nails were loose. *Need to be care*ful, thought Rigo. *Don't want to step on a rusty nail.*

His hand throbbed, reminding him of the events of the night before. He unwound the shirt bandage and inspected it. The blood had dried into a crust, but flexing the hand made the blood flow again. The wound was red and swollen, and warm to the touch. Rigo wondered if that meant it was getting infected. He rewrapped it and decided to inspect the first aid kit he had found in the man's car.

He opened the kit and found bandages of various sizes, some tape, a couple of small packets of antibiotic ointment, two antiseptic wipes, an iodine wipe, a pair of rubber gloves, and a packet of aspirin. He thought for a minute and opened the iodine wipe and, after unwinding the shirt bandage on his hand again, wiped the wound both on the back of his hand and in his palm. He winced and grimaced with its sting. Next, he took a couple of square bandages and bit off pieces of tape to hold them in place. Once done, he ripped off a strip of material from the shirt bandage and tied it around his hand, using his right hand and his teeth, to keep everything in place.

He looked up to find the man watching him.

"You're awake, now, huh?" asked Rigo. "Did you sleep good?" Rigo's laughter stopped the minute he looked at the man's eyes.

"OK, you're probably thirsty. No yelling, OK?" Rigo moved toward the man. "Remember, I've still got my friend here," he pulled the switchblade from his right pocket, "and your gun."

The man nodded and blinked. Rigo loosened the cord tying his hands to his feet and pulled him into a sitting position and yanked the sock from the man's mouth.

The man licked his parched lips and whispered, "Thank you."

Rigo pulled the man by his shoulders so that he could sit propped up against the wall.

"I found some water in your trunk." Rigo walked over to one of the plastic gallon containers. "It don't taste too good, but it's all we've got." He popped off the lid and took it to the man. He put the water container next to the man's lips and slowly poured some into his mouth. The man swallowed and coughed.

"You're right, it *is* lousy. It has been in the car too long." The man took several more swallows before he nodded that he'd had enough.

Rigo drank some water himself and put both containers in a shady corner of the shack. He sat next to the door again, resting his right hand on the gun. The two men sat and looked at each other.

Rigo pulled out the knife and began playing with it. The man watched him with a cautious eye.

At last, the man cleared his throat and asked, "How'd you hurt your hand?"

Rigo sneered. "A big shot was playing a game, and I won," he said.

"I'd hate to see what happened to the other guy," the man replied.

"Yeah, well, sometimes the big shots think they can push the rest of us around," Rigo spat out with bitterness. "They underestimate us – we're smarter and stronger than they think." He twirled the knife around and began waving it in the direction of the man, back and forth, like a snake zeroing in on its victim. "Don't underestimate us," he hissed.

Trying to break the spell, the man took a slow breath and said in a quiet voice, "You're a strong and smart guy, I can see that. What do you plan to do next?"

Rigo stared at the man a minute, and then turned to open the man's briefcase and pulled out a writing pad, a pen, and a letter envelope.

Whispering to himself, he said, "Help my brother."

CHAPTER 19

Trey and Rissa sat on the grass in the engineering quad. They watched for a while as a group of young men, many shirtless, tossed a Frisbee back and forth. The sunny day, the cool grass, and the joy of the students engaged in their game made Rissa feel more relaxed than she had in a long time. Her headache and muscle pains had faded into the background of her mind, with only the occasional twinge reminding her of their presence. She glanced at Trey, who was enjoying watching the young men as much as she was. She smiled to herself, and felt glad that she had met this person whom she found so easy to trust, and who seemed to understand her.

"You know, Trey," she said, "I've never felt comfortable talking about my spiritual beliefs with someone before. I mean, my grandmother insisted we attend church together when I was little, but after I left the Church, well, I've really felt I've had to chart my own path."

"Why did you leave the Church?"

"Well, I was raised Catholic, and when I was in high school, I was struck by how women were left out of the power structure, except for Saint Mary, of course. And I didn't like how the ones in power felt they had a say in almost every aspect of my life. It just didn't make sense to me." She sighed. "My grandmother was really upset when I told her one day that I couldn't be a part of a patriarchal institution anymore, but I think she's forgiven me by now." She paused. "I hope."

"I understand," said Trey. "I was raised in a conservative church and when I heard them preach about how I was created wasn't acceptable, and how they treated it like a greater sin than not acting with justice or loving your neighbor, I had to leave, too."

Rissa nodded. "I followed some of the New Age stuff for a while, but I have trouble with the overemphasis on developing oneself at the expense of developing a social conscience."

"That makes sense. I've seen a lot of navel gazers in that crowd who wouldn't cross the street to help someone in need."

Rissa laughed. "That's pretty harsh, but I understand what you mean." She paused and fingered the pendant at her neck. "I did some research a couple of years ago on the meaning of certain symbols, and I found out that the cross has masculine connotations and the circle symbolizes the feminine. That's when I found this Celtic cross." She lifted the pendant for him to see. "I liked it because it unites the cross, the symbol for the masculine impulse to *do*, with the circle, the feminine impulse to *be*. I think it represents a good balance for how to live."

Trey studied the pendant for a minute and said, "You know, the cross has four arms, and the circle represents wholeness or unity. Four in one. Do you think that has something to do with your dream?"

Rissa considered it. "I'm clueless. I'm hoping the Universe will be a bit more clear."

He nodded, cleared his throat and said, "Well, I hate to leave this wonderful scenery," he pointed his head in the direction of the shirtless students, "but there's something I'd like you to see."

They got up, brushed off the grass from their bottoms, and walked toward the art building. Rissa looked at this man beside her and wondered how he could drive a convertible and sit in linen slacks on grassy lawns and never get his clothes wrinkled or have a hair out of place. *Another mystery*, she thought.

They rounded the corner to the front of the art building and Rissa was greeted by a giant sculpture of what looked like an enormous capital M, squashed so that it was both shorter and broader than the original letter. Its two outer legs had attachments, like long, rectangular feet or claws, pointing inward. The dark grey metal cast shadows where a couple of students were napping out of the sun.

"Here's another example of the number four for you, Rissa," said Trey. "It's called 'The Fourth Sign.'"

"I don't get it."

"The fourth astrological sign – Cancer the crab."

Rissa stared at it for a minute. "I can see the crab, I guess."

"I took a class in the history of astrology at Indiana University, and the sign Cancer fits with what you were talking about in your pendant."

Rissa could see he was ready to expound for a while, so she said, "Let's sit, Professor."

"You see," Trey's hands were already painting pictures in the air, "Cancer is the sign of the summer solstice, which is, what, three days away?" Rissa nodded. "And the solstice is the symbol of the mystic marriage of the sun and the moon."

"Wait, I thought the summer solstice was the celebration of the longest day and shortest night. Isn't marriage about equality?" asked Rissa.

"Yes, but it is also when the sun must relinquish its power as the nights grow longer and longer."

She nodded. "I can see that."

"In ancient times, the priest, who portrayed the sun god, ritually coupled with the priestess, who was portraying the moon or the Divine Mother, before his symbolic death."

"So the sun represents the male energy and the moon the female energy."

"Right," answered Trey, "and the instant that the male energy 'gives up,' which is a female attitude, and the female energy 'moves forward,' which is a male attitude, they are united. A mystical marriage where the two must become like the other in order to become one."

"So you're saying it's really a celebration of how the male and female energies in each sex must come into balance before the two sexes are united?"

Trey nodded.

Rissa continued, "And it's how I view my pendant, the balance of *doing* and *being*."

Trey's hands twittered in the air for a second before he clasped them together. "Oh, I love how you put things together," he said with a broad smile.

CHAPTER 20

Rigo's stomach growled. "Man, I gotta get us some food. You got some money?"

Before the man could answer, Rigo got up, roughly pushed the man over onto his side, extracted his wallet from his right rear pocket, and pushed the man back into a sitting position against the wall.

"Let's see here," said Rigo. He opened the wallet, found a driver's license, some photos of a group of what appeared to be family members from several generations, a photo of a pretty woman with two smiling children and one of a family of four that didn't include the man sitting nearby, an insurance card, an auto club card, three crisp twenty dollar bills and a couple of ones.

"Take what you need," said the man.

Rigo laughed. "I already have," he said.

He piled the papers and pen on top of the brief case, saying, "I gotta eat first. I'll do this later."

He took the wallet and put it in his own back pocket. Standing, he grabbed the man's sock from the floor and shook it once before stuffing it back inside the man's mouth. He pushed the man back onto his side, tightened the cord to bind the man's hands and feet together, double-checked the man's ties to see that they were secure and grunted with satisfaction. Picking up the gun as he walked toward the doorway, he once more admired its heft and small size before putting it in his waistband. He stood in the doorway for a moment and pulled his wrinkled tee shirt down so that it covered both the gun and the bloodstains on his left pocket.

"I'll see you later. Be good," Rigo said as he left.

It was already pushing past the hundred degree mark although it was not yet ten in the morning. *Not only do we need food, but we'll need more water*, thought Rigo.

He looked at the rear of the car and frowned. He went back to the shack, returning with a nearly-empty container of water, and emptied it into the dirt at his feet. He stooped down, mixed the water into the dirt to make it muddy, picked up a handful of mud and wiped it over the license plate. He didn't know if the man was reported as missing yet, but he didn't want to take too many chances.

Wiping his hands on his jeans, he got in the car and drove off.

He soon joined the other travelers heading toward the city. He drove in the slow lane, avoided eye contact with other drivers and did his best to drive under the speed limit.

At last he reached the outskirts of Phoenix. Rigo sweated and chewed the inside of his cheek. *I've got to get rid of this car*, he told himself. *The closer to the city I go, the more cops there will be.*

He passed Buckeye and the White Tank Mountains. Exits were coming up and he decided to head toward Goodyear. He'd been there a couple of times with Sammy, and remembered where a few places were. *First, the car*, he decided.

A couple miles north of the highway sprawled a large shopping area with huge boxy stores, discount outlets, restaurants, and a multiplex movie theater. Rigo parked the car on the outer edge of the parking area and walked toward the movie theater. He slowed his pace, watching people as they went toward the theater. He noticed a group of three teenage girls leave their silver two-door Nissan under a scraggly mesquite tree. Laughing and talking at once, they didn't notice the short, wiry youth eyeing them from behind a minivan. *They'll go to a movie, have lunch, and then shop until late in the afternoon*, Rigo figured. *By that time, I'll be long gone.*

They also were kind enough to leave the window down, he noted. He waited until they bought their movie tickets and entered the theater before he moved toward their car. Looking around, he stood still until he saw that nobody was nearby and jammed his hand inside the window, reached down to unlock the door, and climbed in. He breathed a sigh of relief that there was no alarm on the car. The car smelled of overly sweet perfume and bubblegum lip gloss. Snorting at the pungent mixture of scents, he rolled the window down all the way. Next, he reached underneath the steering column and hotwired the car, a skill he learned courtesy of his friend Sammy. It sputtered to a start. He sat for a minute, looking at the gas gauge. The dial stopped near the full mark. *It really is my lucky day*, he thought.

Rigo drove a couple of blocks and parked at a grocery store. Inside, he bought eight plastic gallons of water, a bundle of thick twine, a small bottle of rubbing alcohol, two boxes of soda crackers, two packets of string cheese, four small bags of beef jerky, and a bunch of bananas. He kept his left hand in his pocket as he paid the cashier and avoided looking at her face. For all she knew, he could have been a day laborer buying supplies for his buddies at the work site. He mumbled his thanks as he drove his cart toward the car, unloaded its contents into the back seat, and drove off.

By the time he'd returned to the weather-beaten shack in the hills, the sun had just passed its apex. Far off, he saw a trio of buzzards trace lazy circles in the clear blue sky. The air pulsed hot and dry; it reminded him of how his mother used the oven to heat the kitchen on cold days in Denver. No chance of rain. June was the month of high temperatures, too early for the more humid days and less intense heat of the monsoon season. Today felt like it could break records.

He wiped the sweat off his face with his sleeve and unloaded the groceries into the shack.

"I'm home," Rigo said.

The man was groggy from the heat. His face shone with sweat and every so often he would move his head to shake off the flies that landed on his cheeks and chin. He watched Rigo bring the food and water in and nodded when Rigo asked if he'd like some water.

Rigo removed the sock from the man's mouth, picked up the gallon-sized container of water he'd already drunk from while driving back, and filled the man's mouth. The man drank nearly a quarter of the container before Rigo stopped. "We gotta save some," he said.

The man nodded, licked his lips, and cleared his throat. "Thanks," he said in a hoarse voice.

Rigo took out his knife, cut off pieces of cheese and jerky and alternated feeding small pieces to the man and biting off large chunks for himself. They both had a few crackers and ended with half a banana each. He allowed the man a couple more mouthfuls of water before he put all the food and water in the shadiest part of the shack and stuffed the man's mouth with the sock.

"Now, to work," Rigo said.

He took the notepad with the printed heading, "From the desk of David Ezker, mayor" and began to write using big, block letters. He had to stop now and then to shoo away flies that were attracted to his sweaty face. The man watched him and squinted as he tried to read the words on the page. Rigo finished the letter and sat, rereading it a couple of times before snorting with satisfaction. He put it aside and sat studying the man with a piercing stare.

"I need something from you," he said.

Rigo walked over to the man and searched his neck for a necklace, but found none. Then, he lay the man over onto his left side with a rough push and looked at the man's hands. He saw what he wanted, a small ring, on the man's fifth finger of his right hand. He twisted the man's hand to get a better look at it. It was a gold school ring from the University of Arizona with a dark blue stone in the middle of it. He tried pulling the ring off, but because of the heat and having been tied up for so long, his fingers were too swollen to remove it. Rigo grunted.

Sometimes you have to do what you have to do, he told himself.

With his left foot, he pushed the man face down, and knelt with his left knee on the man's back. With one swift motion, he took the man's finger and broke it just above where the ring was, near the knuckle. The man bellowed through the sock in his mouth, a guttural, animal sound. Rigo pulled the switchblade from his right front pocket and opened it with a click. The man began to plead, "No, no, no" in desperate tones through his gag, but the words sounded like a hoarse, "Oh, oh, oh." The man was writhing underneath him and Rigo shifted his position to put more weight onto the man. "Stay still," he hissed. Rigo felt for where the broken bone was. He tensed his mouth and commanded his insides to be as still as a glacial lake. He placed the knife underneath the break and sliced upward in a quick, vicious motion.

The man screamed.

Rigo stood up holding the severed finger in his hand, its ring smeared with blood.

Time to put my plan in action, he thought.

CHAPTER 21

"You know, looking at your pendant, I was thinking about something I learned while studying Hermeticism at Washington State University."

Rissa and Trey had sat down for lunch at the student union. Several other diners were seated around the room, some engaged in lively discussions, others in romantic whispers, and a few solitary people busy at their laptops while chewing their food with distraction. Trey had judged the seafood salad as being palatable; Rissa took his word for it and ordered one.

They both were a quarter of the way through their salads when Trey brought up Hermeticism.

"OK, Professor," said Rissa between bites, "what the heck is that?"

"Oh, Hermeticism is based on the teachings of Hermes Trismegistus, or Hermes the Thrice-Great, some 36,000 years ago. He's famous for the saying, 'As above, so below.' There are all sorts of mystery schools based on those teachings, the most famous being alchemy. You've heard of alchemy, right?"

Rissa nodded, her mouth full of tangy shrimp and crisp Romaine lettuce. She raised her index finger while she chewed and swallowed. "Isn't that some sort of magical form of chemistry? Didn't the Church and Rationalism squelch it?"

"Well, yes, I suppose it has had to go underground. There are still some who practice it." Trey put down his fork, his hands beginning to dance in the air. "But what I was thinking of is one of the medieval offshoots of it called Rosicrucianism. 'Rosi' referring to a rose and 'cruci' meaning the cross. The rosy cross. You usually see it pictured as a cross inside an open rose."

"I've read *The Da Vinci Code*. Let me guess – the rose refers to the feminine principle and the cross to the masculine, right?"

"That's right," Trey said. "But some of the Rosicrucian writings take the symbols further – they believed that the cross referred to the intellect and the rose to the heart. They felt that by uniting knowledge with intuition and love, that they would attain divine wisdom and, as some alchemists believed, escape the wheel of birth and rebirth."

"Whoa. You mean they believed in *reincarnation*?"

Trey nodded. "Yes, there are references in alchemy to reincarnation. It's not such a foreign subject in the Christian world. Even Jesus, in the Book of Thomas, told his followers to 'Watch and pray that you may not be born in the flesh, but that you may leave the bitter bondage of this life.'"

"Oh, you're so impressive. How did you remember that?" asked Rissa.

"Photographic memory, which comes in handy at times." He made a slashing motion with his hands. "Still, the point is – why would Jesus tell his disciples to ask not to be born again in the flesh unless there were reincarnation?"

"You don't hear *that* in church," Rissa said. "But, then, I've never heard of the Book of Thomas, either."

"It's a Gnostic writing. I learned about it while studying comparative religions at the University of Washington."

"Oh, I've heard of the Gnostics. They're this early offshoot of Christianity that was eventually stamped out as heretical."

Trey nodded and continued. "And what is the point of reincarnation, but to eventually unite with the divine – or higher consciousness – or whatever you want to call it, and become part of the One?"

Rissa looked up. "There's that number again."

Trey's hands had stilled as he took a bite of salad. He nodded, chewing, and thought for a moment.

"I think it's a number we all search for," he murmured.

CHAPTER 22

"This is our secret weapon, don't you see?" Madame Solanger had grabbed David Ezker's right fifth finger, shaking it, as he sat on the piano bench in her stuffy studio. Her Parisian accent and bountiful perfume harmonized with her décor. Heavy gold curtains tied back with tasseled cords, expensive pillows with exotic prints, and small oil paintings of her native city all served as her backdrop. While other professors in the music school at the University of Arizona seemed satisfied with a few paintings or a small area rug for their office decoration, Madame Solanger transformed the room into a statement that proclaimed from every corner, *Je suis française*!

David was not a music major, but double majored in political science and psychology. Still, he loved music and wanted to continue studying piano while in college. When David was just a boy, his father had taken a second job so that David could take piano lessons from the parish organist in Henderson. When David's skill level exceeded his first teacher's abilities, his father took a third job on Saturdays so that David would be able to study with a better teacher at Phoenix College. And in college, which he attended with the assistance of a couple of scholarships, David had signed up for half-hour piano lessons once a week. He felt lucky to have been able to study with such a renowned teacher as Madame Solanger.

She had been curled up like a cat, lying on her side, feet tucked up under her on her red velvet chaise lounge. Madame Solanger had been listening to David's rendition of the Schumann "Arabesque" with eyes closed, her mouth pinched as if she were about to kiss the air. When David ended with the slow, benedictory section, he let the final chord shimmer for a moment before releasing his hands and pedal, and placed his hands in his lap. That was when Madame Solanger pounced from her cat-like position and had grabbed his finger.

"It is beautiful, yes, but you must make it sing! To make it sing, you must – ," she straightened his small finger so that it became a point extending from his hand, his wrist, and his arm, "like so – you see? The strength, it comes from here," she said, slapping his elbow and shoulder, "and this little thing, this little finger, it becomes our secret weapon, you know?"

She sat on the piano bench, using her tiny frame to edge him off the seat, and he stood to watch her use her small finger to bring the melody out, to let it sing louder than the rolling accompaniment beneath it. The piece sprang to life in his ears; this was music in three dimensions, so unlike his plain, flat playing. For him, it was like comparing the experiences of gazing at a photograph of a redwood tree with that of standing at the foot of a live sequoia and looking up at its topmost branches silhouetted against the sky.

David had continued playing the piano, even after leaving college and working for a time as a school counselor. Other men escaped their mental pressures with drink, drugs, women, or sports, but David found solace in the world of creating beautiful sounds at the piano. When the ugliness of the world got to him, his music was a reminder that there could be loveliness.

David entered the world of politics, becoming the youngest mayor in his native town's history, and learned about the pressures, the complaints, and the difficult compromises that such a job would bring. Late at night, after an arduous city meeting, David would retire to his modest house and play, allowing the singing melodies to transport him to a place far above the worldly plane, to a state of transcendence.

But now, David Ezker found himself bound, gagged, and lying on the filthy floor of an old abandoned shack, his finger broken and sliced off, his hand doused with rubbing alcohol and crudely bandaged. His head ached both from being hit and from dehydration, his muscles screamed from being bound for so long, the stifling heat made breathing a painful chore, and the temperatures were still climbing toward their late afternoon climax. He did not know when his young captor would return and what the boy would do when he did.

There, with his face in the dust, David Ezker cried.

CHAPTER 23

"Well, Rissa, this has been fun, but I've got to run a few errands this afternoon. May I drive you back to your hotel?" Trey wiped his mouth with a napkin. Although it was a paper napkin, he used it like it was the finest linen. He uncrossed his long legs and stood.

Rissa hesitated, wondering how her stomach would manage to hold her food down while she endured another bout of Trey's driving. Still, she could not afford to splurge on a taxi; her meager resources would have to last another five days.

"Um, sure, that would be great," Rissa said, forcing a smile on her lips. She stood and put her right hand on the edge of the table as she picked up her purse from the floor. At that moment, some of the sun gods who had been playing Frisbee earlier walked by the table, laughing and pushing each other. One of them stumbled and pushed Rissa's chair into the table. Its metal armrest banged into Rissa's small finger. She yelped.

"Oh, sorry," said the young man.

Rissa nodded and bit her tongue. Beads of sweat dotted her brow and she felt faint.

Trey studied her for a moment. "Rissa, are you OK?"

"Give me a moment." She gulped down the feeling of nausea and shock. Cupping the hand gently, she moved the fingers up and down. "I don't think anything's broken," she said.

"Let me see," said Trey. With long, gentle fingers, he probed the joints and soft tissues. He clucked once and said, "You're probably right. It's going to leave a nasty bruise, though. You should put some ice on it when you get to the hotel."

"Thanks, I will," said Rissa. She smiled. "So, did you study medicine or anatomy somewhere?" she asked.

"No, just what I learned at Boy Scout camp." His sidelong glance betrayed the laughter in his eyes. "But maybe I could make it my next topic of study." He pursed his lips. "Where would be fun to do that?"

She followed him to his car and endured another nerve-wracking trip which, due to Rissa's fervent prayers to all the saints she remembered from her years as a Catholic, brought her safely to her hotel.

That night, Rissa stared at herself in the mirror as she was brushing her teeth before climbing into bed. Waves of sadness had been washing over her all afternoon, swamping the feelings of happiness and relaxation that she had found in this lovely place with her lively new friend.

Was it because of the hurt finger? she asked herself. *Was it because I'm alone? Am I missing my work or family?* She could not decide what it was that was bothering her.

She stared at the grief-filled eyes in the mirror. They offered her no answers.

CHAPTER 24

Rissa found herself in a hall of mirrors. She was about ten, and her father brought her to the carnival at the fairgrounds. She had wanted to go to the fun house. Her father's large hand let go of hers as she ran into the building.

Inside, a tall clown took her entry ticket. She looked up at his face. Underneath all the paint and the bulbous red nose, she recognized the lean, handsome face, the blond hair, the dancing hands.

"Are you ready to see yourself, little girl?" the clown asked.

Rissa nodded and entered the hall. Mirrors covered the walls, some making her look tall and gaunt, others making her body squat and fat. She laughed as she bobbed up and down in front of the distorted images of herself.

To her right, a moving figure caught her eye. She walked over to that mirror and stood before it. Behind the mirror was a man, his eyes sad and his dark brown hair matted with sweat.

"Help me," he mouthed. She could not hear his voice.

She touched the mirror, hoping to find a way to help the man. She put both hands flat on the mirror and pushed. At the same time, the man touched the glass on his side, his hands shadowed behind hers. His hands were much larger than hers and she noticed that one hand was bandaged. She looked closer.

Under the bandage, one finger was missing.

"Help me," he mouthed again.

Rissa looked around the glass to see if she could find a way to the place where the man was. Seeing none, she ran around the corner, searching for a door or stairway. Only more mirrors, more images of herself.

She ran back to the man's mirror. "Please help me," he mouthed. His hands slipped off the glass and only his face remained.

"I don't know how! I don't know how to help you!" Rissa shouted.

The man's face started to fade. She looked at his grey-blue eyes and was struck by how gentle they seemed. Gentle, and sad at the same time.

"Help . . ." the man's face vanished.

Rissa woke up with a gasp, drenched with sweat. She sat up for a moment, rubbing her face. Through bleary eyes, she glanced at the clock beside the bed.

One-fourteen, it read.

CHAPTER 25

Rigo drove back to the shack feeling both light-headed and smug. His left hand throbbed with each movement he made and he wondered if he should visit an emergency room to have it sewn up. *No money for that now*, he thought. But as he reviewed his plan yet again in his mind, the smugness returned.

That's all about to change, he told himself.

As he drove on in the darkness of midnight, he thought about his brother Manny who would be coming to live with him and his grandmother soon. *I've got to be the man of the family now*, he thought, *and a man provides for his family.* He knew his grandmother would not be able to afford another mouth to feed, and he reaffirmed that he was doing the right thing.

He remembered who put him in this predicament. His father. The image of his father's face floated in his mind like an overfilled balloon about to burst. That's how his father seemed to him. *Like a ticking bomb – you never knew when it would explode.* And he'd seen his father explode many times. Hitting him, his brothers, but mostly his mother. He'd tried to get in between his mother and his father's flailing fists, but his father, taller and brawnier than Rigo by five inches and fifty pounds, just pushed him into a wall or a corner. There Rigo would lie, crumpled like a rag, covering his ears and eyes so that he could not hear the punches landing on flesh, his mother's begging, the cursing, the tears.

And now she was in a hospital somewhere. Rigo wondered if she was still alive. He felt his throat tighten and a heaviness in his chest. Blinking back tears, he reached over with his right hand and picked up the water jug and swallowed a few mouthfuls.

The water did nothing to quench the anger building in his stomach.

How could my father do this? he cried.

Yet, somehow, in the deepest part of himself, he knew the answer. He'd seen how his father worked hard at his construction jobs, only to be fired with a moment's notice whenever the immigration officials were rumored to be coming around. He had heard of the incidents when his bosses shortchanged his father, paying far less than they had promised. He knew of the times when men at the worksite who were younger and less experienced than his father told him what to do and how to do it, and laughed at him behind his back because they gave him the most menial and demeaning jobs.

Rigo knew where his father's rage came from. *It's from the people in power*, he told himself.

He imagined how he'd been handed this golden opportunity to change that. A little over twenty-four hours ago, he'd taken this powerful man and had turned him into a nobody. A little figure lying in the dust, screaming like a girl when he'd sliced off his finger. Rigo's lips curled in contempt. *And now the man and his power were like nothing.* Rigo had made him that way. He smirked, thinking again of his brilliant plan.

Now, I have the power, he thought.

CHAPTER 26

"Hi, doll," Trey said, air kissing Rissa and touching her shoulder. "How's the hand?"

"Oh, still sore, but it moves." She flexed her right hand in proof.

"Well, at least it's not broken."

He had invited Rissa to lunch, enticing her with tales about a little diner with the most tender mahi-mahi in all of Oahu. Trey had offered to drive them there, but since it was a little less than a mile from her hotel, Rissa said that she'd prefer to walk.

The sky was a topaz blue with no sign of clouds. A gentle breeze ruffled her hair – Trey's seemed impervious to becoming messed up – and Rissa drank in the sweet scents of tropical flowers, ocean breezes, and pineapples. Overhead, seagulls squawked to each other in a lazy kind of bickering. *Everything seems so much more easy-going here*, Rissa thought. She watched the traffic parade by without the urgency and rudeness of other big cities she'd visited. *Even the drivers here are more easy-going.* Rissa glanced at Trey ambling beside her in his perfectly pressed linen trousers and silk shirt, and decided, *well, almost every driver.* Rissa inhaled slowly, inviting the calm atmosphere to enter her troubled mind.

Something's still not right, she acknowledged. *I just wish I knew what it was.*

After a while, Trey steered her toward a white house with sky blue trim on the eaves. A weathered sign above the doorway read, "Lenny's Fish Hut and Bar. You hook 'em, we cook 'em."

"Charming," Rissa said with a laugh.

Trey grabbed a couple of menus from a small table inside the entryway and motioned for her to sit at a table along a wall away from the bar. She gave her head a quick shake and adjusted her bangs before putting a paper napkin in her lap.

The restaurant was dark inside; its main source of light came from the huge TV perched on a shelf above the assorted liquor bottles behind the bar. Several patrons already sat on the vinyl barstools, their rubber-soled boots splattered and stained, their work clothes sweaty and dirty even though it was early afternoon. Rissa wondered if these were the people that had hooked 'em. They seemed in good spirits, or had been imbibing good spirits, and speared their French fries and fried fish with gusto.

Ceiling fans spun in lazy, off-kilter circles above them and a couple of flies buzzed in the soft air currents. Rissa squinted at her menu in the low light and noticed that it had ketchup and coffee stains on its plastic cover. She looked up at Trey, who was watching her with amusement.

"Trust me, it's the best mahi-mahi around. I'll order for us both, OK?"

Rissa nodded. The harried waitress soon came, slammed a couple of small glasses of water on the table, and took Trey's order. Not ten minutes later, the waitress returned with two plastic plates full of grilled mahi-mahi and coleslaw. Rissa took a tentative taste.

"Oh, my God, you're right." She wiped up the juices that threatened to dribble down her chin.

"Told you," said Trey with a Cheshire cat grin.

One of the bar patrons yelled for the TV to be turned up so that they could follow the mid-day news. The waitress grumbled as she grabbed a chair, climbed up on it and punched the volume button several times. The crowd roared their thanks and continued talking, drinking, and eating piles of food.

The news blared on and on about the usual wars, murders, and weather disasters until a story caught Rissa's ear. She turned with interest as the perky young newscaster with the contralto voice intoned, "We bring news of a shocking twist in a missing person's case from Arizona. Coming to you live from our sister station in Phoenix, Arizona is Ana Pilar Guzman, who tells of a gruesome find made by police this morning. Ana Pilar?"

"Yes, thank you, Donna. I am speaking live from the steps of the town hall in Henderson, Arizona, a small town of about 4500 on the southwestern fringes of the Phoenix metropolitan area. Police received a missing person call yesterday morning about its mayor, David Ezker, but this case has taken a gruesome turn with what the police found on the steps of the town hall early this morning."

The broadcast went to a pre-recorded summary. In the background were the modest tan-brick town hall and a trio of police searching the ground for clues. A yellow "police line, do not cross" tape was stretched behind Ana Pilar, who held a microphone in front of a man in uniform identified as the chief of police, Edgar Robles.

The interview started with him speaking in mid-sentence. " . . . this morning. We found an envelope with a letter on city stationery demanding a large sum of money, and enclosed with the letter was a severed finger with a ring on it."

Ana Pilar moved the microphone to herself as she asked, "And has someone identified the finger or the ring?"

"Yes, our city manager recognized the ring. There was an inscription inside that he recognized."

"Are you considering the Mayor to be a hostage?"

"Yes, this has evolved beyond a missing person's case. The letter made it clear that he is being held for ransom."

"And do you have any leads at this point?"

"Not at this time. We are asking the community to come forward to assist us in solving this case." He provided a phone number for people to contact.

The next shot in the news feed was a photograph of a man with dark hair, a prominent nose, full lips, and gentle blue-grey eyes. The caption underneath identified him as David Ezker, mayor of Henderson, Arizona.

Rissa's fork clattered to the floor. "I know him!" she yelled.

CHAPTER 27

"I really can't take you anywhere," chided Trey, who picked Rissa's fork off the floor and grabbed a clean one from an adjacent table. The bar boys had stopped staring at them and slowly returned their focus to their own plates and the TV.

"No, you don't understand. I've seen that man's face before." Rissa felt hot and flustered.

"I'll bite. What are you talking about?"

"I had a dream last night – a really strange one – and this man was trapped somewhere and he kept asking me for help. I remember his right hand was bandaged and was missing his little finger."

Trey wiped his mouth. "The news report didn't say which hand or which finger it was. Are you sure?"

"Yes! He was trapped behind a mirror and instead of seeing myself, I saw him, and he put his hands up behind mine on the glass and that's when I noticed the missing finger." Rissa gulped. "You know, this is silly. I'm talking about a stupid *dream* here."

Trey studied her. "Not so fast. We could be talking about how you have tapped into the collective unconscious, or maybe a psychic vision, or any number of things. Tell me: have you had any other feelings of connection like this before?"

Rissa leaned back in her chair and thought for a long while. At last she said, "It's silly."

"Don't shut down on me. Tell me. After all, this man is being held by someone who has at least a knife and, in a dream, this man appealed for help. To *you*, I might add. And you know what they say, 'There are no coincidences.'" He cleaned his fingers with his napkin and crossed his arms.

Rissa bit her lip. She glanced at Trey's lean face. With downcast eyes, she said, "Well, I still feel this is silly, but here goes." She heaved a sigh. "Over the years, ever since I was a little girl, I've been sensitive to how others feel. I could walk into a room and know what others are feeling and sometimes their feelings would overwhelm me. It has taken me a long time to learn how to let go of those feelings."

"So, you're sensitive, and possibly empathic. Go on."

"But there were times when I was alone and I would feel another person's feelings. They were from nobody I knew, and from nobody I'd been in contact with, but they were feelings that I knew weren't mine even though I felt them. Does this make sense?" Rissa's eyes were pleading.

Trey nodded.

"I mean, I can tell when the feelings aren't mine. It's like wearing another person's sweater. It doesn't fit."

"I think I understand," Trey offered.

"Anyway, in the last few years, I've felt more than just feelings." Rissa paused, biting her lip. "And I think it always comes from the same person. I call him my invisible friend."

She smiled to herself. "Sometimes, it was music I'd hear in my head. Either music from the radio or else piano music that I didn't recognize. Classical music. Other times, it would be a quick image in my mind, like a photograph. Sometimes I'd see a flash of a sunset, or a mountain range, or a child's little shoe lying in the street. Nothing that I'd seen before was specific as that." Tears welled in her eyes. She stared at her hands in her lap. "You probably think I'm crazy," she whispered.

Trey reached over and touched her arm. His eyes bored into her face until she would return his gaze.

"No, Rissa, I don't think you're crazy." His voice was soft. "I think you've been in contact with your twin soul."

CHAPTER 28

"Well, Professor, you're going to have to explain yourself. What is a twin soul?" Rissa's eyes held both pain and annoyance.

The dancing hands were already aloft. "It was Plato who first wrote about it in his *Symposium*, 4th century B.C.E. He said that there were originally three kinds of humans: men, women, and androgynous. But because these humans were so proud and strong, the gods felt threatened and so Zeus decided to split each human in half."

"Androgynous?"

"Equally male and female. So when that soul was split, its male half desired its female half."

Rissa smiled. "Like all the plot lines in romantic movies."

"Right. And the female searched for its other female half, and the male for its other male half." Trey lowered his eyes.

"I bet they don't teach this in the Bible belt."

"Ah, no. I learned about it at Princeton, actually." He smiled. "But according to Plato, it is the soul's life quest to find its other half."

Trey tilted his head as he searched for the page in his mind's eye. "'So ancient is the desire of one another which is implanted in us, reuniting our original nature, making one of two, and healing the state of man.'"

Rissa's eyes grew wide. "'Making one of two'? Like the 'one plus one equals one' in my dream?"

Trey's hands froze in midair. "Oh, my God. It never occurred to me . . ." His hands fell in his lap, as if invisible puppeteer's strings were suddenly severed.

"And the number four means completion, wholeness. So, completion is found when one plus one equals one. Wow." Rissa's eyebrows rose beneath her bangs.

"Even Jesus had a twin soul, you know." Trey's eyes were twinkling.

"Let me guess: Mary Magdalene."

"Well, according to one of the Gnostic texts, no. Guess again."

"John, the beloved disciple?"

"No. According to the Book of Thomas, it was Thomas himself."

"You mean Doubting Thomas?" Rissa shot him a dubious look.

"That was a moniker given to him later by those who wanted to portray him as being outside Jesus' circle of confidantes. Actually, the other disciples were jealous of the secret things Jesus taught Thomas." Trey paused. "Thomas means 'twin,' you know."

He searched his mental library. "Jesus said to Thomas: 'Since it is said that you are my twin and my true friend, examine yourself and understand who you are, how you live, and what will become of you.'"

"That sounds like he's telling Thomas that they are on parallel paths."

"And *that*, my friend, has an interesting parallel in the world of physics."

"You studied physics? I'm impressed."

"Kansas State University. Anyway, have you heard of quantum entanglement?"

"Quantum, yes, the other part, no." Rissa frowned. "Is this going to make my brain hurt?"

"I'll give you the condensed version." His hands were poised to illustrate. "When scientists split a photon – which is a small wave-particle of light – into two equal parts, the two parts are considered entangled. They do interesting things. When the scientists change the polarization of one of the particles, the other one changes *at the exact same moment*."

"You mean the scientists affects both by only changing one?"

"That's right. And it happens at the very same instant no matter how far apart the two particles are."

"My brain is starting to hurt."

"Well, it affected Einstein the same way. He called quantum entanglement 'spooky action at a distance.'" Trey laughed.

"That *is* spooky." Rissa paused to think. "So, I see how this explains how I can sense my twin soul across distances – if indeed that's what is going on with me, and not insanity," Rissa added with ruefulness. "But are there examples in nature about things joining? I mean, you see things splitting all the time – one human egg into twin babies, atoms, branches off a tree – but what about things coming together?"

Trey nodded. “At the University of Utah, I learned about chimera.”

Rissa gave him a look of being lost.

“You mentioned human eggs splitting to form twins. A chimera is formed when two fertilized eggs, fraternal twins, join together. It creates a baby with two different sets of chromosomes. I’ve seen pictures of babies who have noticeably different skin coloring, a lighter one on, say, the left side of the body, and a slightly darker one on the right. There’s a line running down the middle where the skin color changes.”

“But since I’ve not ever seen anyone like that, this condition must be rare.”

“Well, perhaps not as rare as we might think. You know how all calico cats are supposed to be female?”

“I grew up with a cat that was a male calico. Pretty rare, I was told, but the vet said it happens now and then.”

“Your cat may have been a chimera. Female coloring with male sex organs. Two sets of chromosomes joined.”

“Interesting.”

“And then there’s nuclear fusion.”

“More brain pain?” Rissa asked.

“Well, I hope not.” Trey’s hands formed two balls. “The sun creates heat, light, radiation, and energy through fusion.” His two hands united to create one ball. “It’s when two hydrogen atoms join, creating a helium atom plus a neutron. Not a perfect example, but I like the metaphor of two becoming one and bringing light on the subject.”

Rissa groaned and began poking at her cold mahi-mahi. She put a forkful in her mouth, hummed at the delicious flavor, and looked at Trey with a piercing gaze.

“Last question, Professor.” Her look was serious. “What do we do now?”

Trey motioned while he finished chewing. “For once, I don’t have an answer for you.”

CHAPTER 29

Walking back to the hotel, Rissa's eyebrows drew together in puzzlement. "You know, Trey, there's something I don't understand. And I want to ask you about it without giving offense."

It was Trey's turn to raise his eyebrows. "Oh, you don't have a mean bone in your body. What's your question?"

"Well, when you said that the Book of Thomas identified Thomas as being Jesus' twin soul, does that mean that Jesus was homosexual?"

To Rissa's relief, Trey laughed. "I don't think so. The premise of *The Da Vinci Code*, that Jesus was married to Mary Magdalene, is still possible." He grabbed her arm as they crossed a street. "And believe it or not, I *do* research things that interest me outside of school. In my private reading, I've learned that people don't always reincarnate as one sex only. They may be a man in one life, a woman in the next, and so on. I think that gender and the essence of the soul are two different things."

"OK, so Plato's theory that there are female souls and male souls and ambidextrous souls . . ."

"Androgynous," Trey corrected.

"Right. *Androgynous* souls – really refers to the inner person, no matter what body they live in for that lifetime." Rissa flailed her hands as she thought of how to word her question. "So, how do you know what the gender of your inner soul is?"

"That's a good question. I'm going to answer your question with a question."

"Go ahead."

"What do you think of when I say 'male'?"

Rissa thought for a moment. "I'd say the active force."

"Yes," nodded Trey, "and it is typically associated with the sun, right?"

"I remember hearing that."

"And what do you think of when I say 'female'?"

"The passive force. And isn't the female associated with either the moon or the Earth? You know, 'Mother Earth'?"

"That's right." Trey smiled. "And in some ancient writings, the sun referred to the heavenly and the eternal, while the Earth stood for the carnal and the mortal."

"Maybe that explains why women have been treated so badly over the centuries." Rissa frowned. "Still, I'm not sure I see how this answers my question . . ."

"Then listen to this." His eyes rolled upward as he searched his mental library. "I'll paraphrase first. In the Gospel of Thomas . . ."

"You mean the Book of Thomas?"

"Same guy, different book." He took an exaggerated breath, looked at her with mocking eyes and continued, "*As I was saying* . . . In the Gospel of Thomas, Jesus was with his disciples and they were watching some babies nursing. Jesus said that those who are like those nursing babies will enter the kingdom of heaven. The disciples asked Jesus if they could only enter the kingdom as babies."

"I've heard that story before. In the Gospel of John, I think. Except it was some guy named Nicodemus who asked the question."

"That happens a lot, when you have a similar story in different gospels. And in the Gospel of John, Jesus answered that one must be born of water and the spirit."

"Yes, I remember that."

"But listen to what Jesus answers in the Gospel of Thomas. 'When you make the two into one, and when you make the inner like the outer and the outer like the inner, and the upper like the lower, and when you make male and female into a single one, so that the male will not be male nor the female be female . . . Then you will enter the kingdom.'"

"Hey, he talked about making the two into one!" Rissa grinned at the recognition.

"And I think that there are two other very important parts to this quote. The first one is when he talks about making the upper like the lower. In other words, he says it is necessary to join the mortal with the divine."

"OK, I think I follow." Rissa's lips twisted in puzzlement. "And the second important part?"

"When he says that the male should no longer be male and the female no longer female. In other words, your internal gender really doesn't matter. What *is* important is the need to balance the active and the passive parts of yourself. "

Rissa blew out a long breath. At last, she said, "You've given me a lot to think about." She hugged his arm. "Thanks, Professor."

They walked another block before Rissa spoke again.

"Trey, I hope you don't mind me asking, but do you have a twin soul you know about?"

His full lips pinched as if in pain. His voice was quiet. "Yes, there was a young man that I *knew* . . ."

"You recognized his essence as being your other half?"

Trey nodded.

"What happened? I mean, you don't have to tell me if you don't want to talk about it."

Trey rubbed his mouth and gave her a small smile. "No, it's all right. He was a fellow student, an English major, at the University of Chicago. Chris and I connected in ways I can't describe. It was like I could read his thoughts and he could read mine, and just sitting in silence with him was as fulfilling as hours spent in conversation with other people."

"Is he still in Chicago?"

"No. Chris died, actually." The look of pain returned to his face. "It was stupid, really. He was killed in an auto accident. A brilliant mind, a beautiful soul, cut short by something like that." His mouth twisted. "What a waste."

"But you still miss him."

"Oh, yes." His eyes grew big with wonder. "But the funny thing is that I still feel him, every day. Like we were continuing our silent conversations." His eyes looked down. "But yes, I miss him, too."

Rissa thought for a moment. *Now I understand why he drives like a kamikaze*, she thought. *He wants to be together again.*

They continued walking in silence until they reached the hotel. As they entered the lobby, she turned to Trey and said, "Professor, I've decided what I need to do."

"What's that?"

"I need to make a phone call to the chief of police in Henderson, Arizona."

CHAPTER 30

David Ezker tensed as he heard the young man drive up to the shack, get out of the car, slam the door and enter the building. The boy's heavy steps made the floor boards he was lying on slap his face.

It was late afternoon, and the sun was at its hottest, baking the already scorched land. The boy had been away most of the night, returned to give David some water and a little food early that morning, and afterward left again for most of the day. He wondered where he'd gone.

David eyed the young man's face. He was whistling softly, and seemed pleased with himself. David figured that the boy had delivered some sort of ransom note with his finger as proof. David wondered where he delivered the note.

"Time to eat." The boy loosened the rope binding David's hands to his feet and roughly pulled him into a sitting position. David flexed his stiff thighs as much as he was able. He yearned to be able to move his aching arms and shoulders. He wanted to see his hand.

The boy yanked the sock out of David's mouth. David rocked his jaw back and forth and then closed his mouth to recover some moisture.

"I bet you want some water." The young man grabbed one of the plastic gallon containers of water and trickled some into his mouth. "Take it easy, we've got to make this last." David gulped down three or four more mouthfuls before the boy pulled the jug away.

The young man began cutting slices of jerky into bite-sized bits; it was nearly gone. He fed the jerky and some crackers piece by piece, as if he were feeding a young child. David stole glances to study the boy's face. It was sweaty and stubble grew above his lip and in patches on his jaws. A slight case of adolescent acne dotted his forehead. His eyes were hard.

After a couple more swigs of water, David spoke. "Thank you."

The boy looked at him and snorted.

"My name is David. I'd like to know what to call you." David's voice was hoarse.

The boy stared at David for a moment, thinking. "You can call me Peter, 'cuz I'm a rock," he said, hitting his chest with a closed fist.

"OK, Peter, I was wondering if I might stretch my shoulders, or at least look at my hand. I'm worried it might be getting infected."

Peter sat and considered the idea. "No way. You're like gold to me. I can't risk you taking off."

David nodded. "Would you mind looking at my hand? It's feeling really hot and sore."

"That's 'cuz I cut your stupid finger off!" The boy called Peter laughed. Once he caught the look in David's eyes, he grew solemn. He grabbed the first aid kit and the rubbing alcohol and gently removed the bandage on David's hand. He poured more alcohol on it, which made David gasp with pain, rubbed it with the last antibiotic pad and re-bandaged it.

"Thank you." David's voice was a whisper.

"Yeah, it's red, but I'll keep an eye on it. I need you alive for another thirty-two hours." Peter yawned. "I'd really like to take a nap. And I need you to shut up." He reached for the sock and stuffed it back into David's mouth. David cringed at the feeling of grit in his mouth.

Peter rolled David on his side and tightened the rope tying his feet to his hands. David's muscles screamed in protest.

Peter sat against the wall nearest the door, the pistol near his right hand, and closed his eyes. David heard the boy's breaths grow louder and slower as he fell asleep.

David needed to focus his thoughts away from his pain and worry. He closed his eyes and began counting his breaths, a discipline he'd learned in college whenever the stress of deadlines got to him. It was a technique that served him well when he felt overwhelmed by the pressures of leadership. That, and his music.

No, I can't think about that right now. He pushed the beloved melodies out of his mind and refocused on his breath. In, out. In, out. His breathing slowed and his muscles relaxed a bit.

Somewhere between consciousness and unconsciousness, an image began to form in his mind. It grew slowly, as if he were looking through a peephole, but it soon emerged and filled his whole inner vision. It was an ocean scene, with soft white sand and palm trees towering at the edge of the beach. He could see a gentle breeze ruffle the edges of the palm fronds and overhead he noticed seagulls flying in slow patterns. He noticed tropical flowers off to the side – hibiscus and bird of paradise – and imagined that the scent would be sweet. The ocean rolled in and out, and David's breaths matched the rhythm of the waves.

With a slight smile at the corners of his lips, he drifted off to sleep.

CHAPTER 31

"Jeez, I wish we'd written down the number from the news report," said Rissa with the phone planted at her ear. She and Trey were in her hotel room, having waded through directory assistance and then the Henderson city government for the phone number to the chief of police. Rissa tried out various opening lines in her mind, not sure of how to speak to the officer about the psychic contact she had with her twin soul who was being held for ransom. *He's going to think I'm a crackpot*, she thought.

When the phone line to the police department rang at long last, Rissa's mind went blank.

"Henderson Police," a gruff voice said.

Rissa thrust the phone at Trey. He shot her a look of annoyance, but recovered and spoke in tones as smooth as his silk shirt.

"Ah, yes, officer, we may have some information about your missing Mayor."

"And who is calling, please?" asked the voice.

"This is Irving Waverly the third with Clarissa Wright. We're calling from the island of Oahu and . . ."

"Look, mister, we don't have time for honeymooners' pranks. Why don't you get off the line and let those here in Arizona help us out?" The voice grew louder with each word.

"Well, Officer . . ?" Trey let the hesitation linger.

"Officer Cano," the voice offered at last.

"Well, Officer Cano, my friend here has some information that would tell you whether she could be of help or not." Trey passed the phone to Rissa.

"Um, hi, Officer Cano," Rissa said, "I had a dream . . ."

The officer sighed loudly.

" . . . a dream where I saw this man and he lost a finger."

"Yeah, we told everyone in the nation he lost a finger, missy," said Officer Cano.

"But you didn't say which."

"OK, you tell me which finger and I'll tell you whether I'm going to listen to you any longer." Officer Cano's tone told her he was close to hanging up.

"It was his right hand little finger. There was a gold ring with a blue stone on it from his school, and there's an inscription inside that says, '*Spero melior.*'"

There was a long pause. Trey watched Rissa as she listened, nodded her head, and said, "OK" and "uh-huh" a few times. At long last she hung up the phone and looked at Trey.

"Well?" he asked.

"He wants to know when we can be in Arizona."

CHAPTER 32

"Trey, I want to thank you for everything – I mean, you've made arrangements with the airline, you're taking me to the airport, you've done so much . . ." Rissa's voice choked with emotion.

"And I'm going with you," Trey glanced at her as he passed two cars on the right while going fifteen miles over the speed limit.

"What?"

"I said, I'm going with you. It's all arranged. I'm calling it 'field research' and billing everything to dear old Dad." He grinned.

"You're too much," she said with a laugh. Her laughter faded as she questioned herself, *Why does he still want to be with me? Why is it so important to him to see how the story ends?* She shrugged. *Perhaps it is all an intellectual game, some way to prove that his research has some real-life application.* She decided that time would tell.

Trey had booked two seats in first class on the overnight flight to Phoenix. Sitting in her seat, Rissa ran her hand over the smooth tan leather and stretched her legs out as far as she could in front of her.

"I could get used to this," she said, grinning.

While savoring a dinner of steak *au poivre,* asparagus, warm whole wheat rolls, and a mixed salad, Rissa asked, "Trey, I've been thinking about all you've told me and there's something I don't fully understand."

"Ask away."

"Could you explain more about your point that 'the upper like the lower' means that the human and divine must unite?"

Trey finished chewing, put down his knife and fork, and wiped his mouth with a flourish with his white cloth napkin. "Do you know what astrological sign we're in right now?"

"What? No." Rissa looked puzzled.

"We're in Gemini, the sign of the twins."

"Interesting – twins."

"More interesting is the Greek myth associated with this sign."

Rissa prepared herself for a lecture. "Go on, Professor."

"According to some versions of the myth, the god Zeus became enamored with Leda, the beautiful wife of a king, and in order to seduce her, turned himself into a swan. She conceived and gave birth to two sets of twins – two boys and two girls."

"Wait. I thought that Gemini was only about one set of twins."

"That's the common understanding. But in this myth, the twin boys were Castor and Pollux . . ."

"I've heard of them."

Trey nodded, ". . . and the twin girls were Helen and Clytaemnestra. It's interesting because each pair of twins has one mortal child and one immortal. Both Pollux and Helen were considered demigods, where Castor and Clytaemnestra were fully human."

"It's like a double duo: mortal and divine males and mortal and divine females."

"Exactly. And in their own way, both sets of twins represent the challenges of uniting the upper and lower aspects of personality."

Rissa's eyebrows knit together. "Go on."

"Take, for example, the girl twins: Helen and Clytaemnestra. Helen is the divine one, and her passivity and lack of initiative helped ignite the Trojan War."

"Oh, she's Helen of Troy! I've heard of her, too." Rissa smiled.

"Yes, but her mortal sister represents the shadow side of the will. Where Helen was passive to the extreme, Clytaemnestra was ruled by her passions and eventually murdered her husband, King Agamemnon, when he returned from the Trojan War. So, you see, only when the will is balanced by a higher vision can destruction be averted."

"Meaning . . . ?"

Trey paused a moment, lips pursed. "I think it means that action needs to be bonded with reflection. When we decide to take action, our actions need to be guided by a higher vision. We need to consider the consequences of everything we do – to ourselves, our relationships, our environment, the future – when we decide to act. Our world can't afford to be ruled by emotions or narrow-mindedness anymore."

Rissa nodded. "I think I understand that better now. But what about the twin boys?"

"What do you think the hardest part of being a human or divine twin would be?"

Rissa thought for a moment. "Probably the fact that the mortal one would eventually die and they would be apart."

"Yes. Eternal separation. In the myth of Castor and Pollux, Castor *was* killed, in battle. Since the twins had hardly ever been apart, Pollux was heartbroken. So, Pollux begged his father Zeus to let him die so he could be with his brother, but that was impossible because he was born immortal. So, Zeus decreed that Pollux ascend to heaven where he and his brother could be together eternally. Those are the names of the stars that make up the astrological sign, by the way – Castor and Pollux. Pollux, the divine twin, is the slightly brighter star."

"So, what was the challenge of this set of twins, in terms of uniting the higher and lower parts of the self?"

"Overcoming death and separation."

"And how did they do that?"

"Through the bond of love."

Rissa was quiet as they finished their meal. She thought about Trey's words and wondered if it was that kind of bond that tied her to the Mayor. Was he to mean something to her and become a part of her life? Was this connection something like what she heard about soul mates? Would he fulfill some deep emptiness that she'd felt all her life? Would their relationship signal that they were uniting not only the two halves of their separated soul, but also the higher and lower aspects of their nature?

Her mind wandered as she remembered the three boyfriends she'd had in her life. Being by nature a quiet person, Rissa found romantic relationships difficult. She recalled that her first bout of puppy love, with Justin, had been in junior high, but it didn't last because he decided that she wasn't nearly as interesting as Candi, one of the blond cheerleaders with a well-developed bust line. She pictured how she met her second boyfriend, Dave, in high school, when her father insisted she join the drama club to help overcome her shyness. Tall, funny, and a fine athlete besides, she soon tired of Dave's fondness for burping out the letters of the alphabet or repeating jokes about bodily functions. In her freshman year of college, she met Sam, who was also studying to become a social worker. She soon fell for his quiet, caring ways and how he would focus intently on her when she spoke, making her feel as if she were the most important person in the world to him. Their relationship lasted until spring break, when she found out he was going to San Diego for the week with his friend Bill. The relationship between Sam and Bill was not platonic, she discovered.

She glanced at Trey. It wasn't Sam's sexual preference that bothered her; it was the deceit. It took her a long time to get over the betrayal.

She thought about how her invisible friend – her twin soul – called to her like a beacon. Whether they were meant to be together or not, she hoped that she would be able to help find him. She hoped that she was ready, if he was meant to be in her life. She made that into a prayer and sent it to the Universe.

CHAPTER 33

After dinner, Rissa decided a glass of wine might help her overcome her nervousness about flying and help her sleep as well. She knew it would be a short night and she needed all the rest she could get.

Soon, her head was resting on Trey's shoulder, her mouth open and snoring softly. He looked down at her, sighed, and decided to shut his eyes for a while, too.

Inside Rissa's mind whirled a flurry of images. A racing blue convertible, palm trees, a wooden tiki with human hair, a giant steel crab, her calico cat from childhood, nude infant boys cradling each other in the night sky. At last images slowed until she found herself standing next to a horse, staring at the saddle on its back. The saddle had an exaggerated slope to it because of its tall horn and extra high seat back. It reminded her of an old-fashioned saddle that the conquistadores had used. She wanted to climb up, but the horse kept getting taller and taller until the saddle was beyond her reach. With a loud neigh, the horse reared and bolted away, far to her left.

Next, she was standing in a desert wilderness with mountains in the background. She counted four peaks in the mountain range. A huge sheep with big horns came running into view and stopped before her. Its two horns curled around the sides of its head and it had a ferocious look in its eye. The sheep lowered its head and Rissa wondered if she should run away. The two horns grew thicker until they joined together into one huge, wide horn. The weight of the horn caused the sheep's head to drop lower and lower until its nose touched the ground. The ground gave way and the sheep sank into the soil. At last, the only thing that Rissa could see of the sheep was the slope of its neck and back leading to its powerful brown shoulder.

The next thing she knew, Trey was nudging her arm and saying, "Time to wake up" in a soft voice.

Rissa roused herself with a couple of cups of steaming coffee and a trip to the lavatory to splash water on her face. She looked at Trey and wondered how anyone could look so impeccable after a couple of hours' sleep. Only the dark circles under his eyes betrayed the extent of his weariness.

The last part of the flight into Phoenix was bumpy. Trey noticed Rissa grabbing the arms of the seat like a cat.

"Thermal currents. They're caused by rising heat." He patted her hand.

She looked out the window. "It's so *brown*."

"Yes, but it's lovely in the winter months. Right now is their hot, dry season. And," Trey leaned over to glance at the scenery, "this *is* a desert."

Exiting the plane, Rissa gasped as the dry, oven-like air hit her while taking the step between the plane door and the jet way. *And it's only 7:30 in the morning*, she thought with dread.

Rissa waited at the carousel for their luggage while Trey went to the rental car counter. *I hope he didn't get a convertible*, she thought.

Twenty minutes later, with luggage in tow and rental car keys in hand, Trey motioned for them to sit in a couple of quiet seats. He spread a large detailed map of Arizona in front of her. Rissa's eyes bulged. She had never realized just how big Arizona was.

"Well, Rissa, it's time to put up or shut up. Where do we go from here?"

CHAPTER 34

"I -- I -- I'm not sure," Rissa stammered. "I did have a dream, but it was confusing. I don't know if it had anything to do with *this,"* she said, pointing to the map before them.

Rissa quickly related the dream to Trey, who listened intently and nodded his understanding.

"So, the first thing you saw was a horse. A tall horse, right? Hmm," he said, studying the list of place names on the side of the map, "there's a Dead Horse Ranch State Park *here*." He pointed to an area between Clarkdale and Cottonwood, southwest of Flagstaff.

"I don't know. It doesn't feel right. I think the area we're looking for isn't so green."

"That's the map, silly. It just shows that it's in a national forest area."

"Well, I guess we're looking for something that's not a forest." Rissa paused. "I think. It felt more like a desert."

Trey studied her. He could feel their tiredness. He lowered his voice to project calm. "All right, tell me how you knew about the ring on the guy's finger. You never explained that to me."

Rissa thought a moment. "I just was talking to the officer, and a picture of it popped into my head, and as I was speaking to him, the words just came out. I don't even know what the inscription means, or what language it's in."

"I believe it's Latin. I know that *spero* means 'I hope' or 'I wish' and *melior* means 'better,' if I recall correctly. Perhaps it could be translated as, 'I hope for better things' or something like that. Anyway," Trey brushed some lint off his trousers, "after the horse in your dream disappeared, what came next?"

"A mountain range with four peaks in it."

"That's easy. There's a Four Peaks Wilderness just northeast of here." He pointed to the map.

"And after the horse ran away behind me and the mountains came into view, there was a big sheep or goat with two horns that eventually grew into one."

"What kind of sheep or goat?"

"It reminded me of the bighorn sheep you see in the Rockies, except with a smaller build."

"Perhaps there are bighorns here in Arizona, too. We'll need to ask about that."

Trey started to fold the map. "I suggest we start with going to the police department in Henderson, which is *here*," he pointed on the map section which he left open, "and then hope that you'll get the information we need at the time we need it." He handed her the map, grabbed their suitcases, and started for the exit. Rissa trotted along behind him.

Soon they were traveling west on I-10, going through the downtown area. Trey was speeding as usual, but Rissa was glad that their rental car did not have the horsepower that his BMW did. Traffic was heavy as well, which also slowed him down. It made reading the map spread on her lap easier.

"Trey, what should I expect to feel when I meet my twin soul, I mean, assuming that we find him and everything. What was it like for you?"

Trey passed a slow-moving semi and glanced at her. "For some people, as it was for me, it was like meeting my best friend after a long separation. For others, they recognize in the other person some part of themselves that they can't stand and the relationship blows apart. In the movies, of course, they portray it as love at first sight, goo-goo eyes and all that." Rissa giggled. "But I really think it all depends on you."

"What do you mean by that?" Rissa asked.

Trey took a long breath. "You remember me mentioning alchemy, right?"

Rissa nodded.

"As you may know, alchemy is the ancient study of the process of turning lead into gold. There are seven steps to this process. Did you know that?"

Rissa said she didn't.

"The fourth step is conjunction, in which there is a four-way uniting. Think of a cross. The horizontal axis refers to the marriage of the sun and the moon, which is often portrayed as a King and Queen coming together in marriage or in sexual union."

Rissa nodded.

"The vertical axis refers to the union of the spirit above and matter below." Trey motioned toward her necklace. "The symbol for conjunction is a bit like your pendant, actually. It is a cross with a circle on top of the vertical axis, rather like the Egyptian ankh."

Rissa's eyebrows were drawn together in thought. "Let me see if I get this right. You're saying that it's like our two sets of

Gemini twins. The horizontal axis, as you say, is like the twin girls learning to balance feminine passivity with masculine willfulness."

"That's right." Trey smiled.

"And the vertical axis refers to the boy twins who had to unite the mortal with the divine."

"Very good," Trey gushed. "In fact, some researchers liken the fourth alchemical step, conjunction, to the ancient ritual of *hieros gamos*, which comes from ancient Mesopotamia. It was the public sexual union of the king and the sacred prostitute. To them, it represented both the union of the male and female essences, and also the mortal and the divine."

Rissa glared at him.

"University of California at Northridge, world religions," Trey offered.

"Well, I still don't understand how all this knowledge applies to your statement that how it will feel to meet my twin soul depends all on me."

"Because alchemy is not just about physical lead and physical gold. It is an internal process as well." His voice was gentle. "So, how you have learned to balance your masculine and feminine essences and your mortal and spiritual selves really *does* affect everything." His right hand was pointing. "The most famous saying in alchemy is, 'As above so below; as below so above; as within so without; as without so within.'"

"So, you're saying that in order to be united with my twin soul, I need to be united and balanced within myself."

"That's my understanding."

"And assuming that I am balanced horizontally and vertically, and assuming I do find my twin soul, what then?"

"Well, according to my research, *if* you are ready, and *if* he is ready, then you unite and when you die, you evolve to become a male-female pair."

“Wait. You’ve mentioned this before, in Hawaii, at the museum. What was it called?”

“An ‘aumakua. A mother-father guardian spirit. Using all their life experiences, they join to help another pair of souls through the school of life.”

Rissa sighed. “You know, Trey, that’s a lot of "if’s". Let’s find the man first.”

Trey nodded. “Agreed.”

CHAPTER 35

Officer Ray Cano was having a very bad day. His boss, Chief Robles, was displeased with him because he had invited two strangers claiming to be psychics into the confusion involving the Mayor. *'Displeased' is probably too gentle a term*, Cano thought. He had not seen Chief's face turn that shade of red since a group of teens had toppled the radio tower above the station.

So, Cano spent most of the morning avoiding standing anywhere near the Chief. That was made difficult because the Feds, who had invited themselves into the case, used Cano's desk as their headquarters. *I can't even hide behind my desk*, he sulked.

Having the Feds around was enough to give anyone a headache, but Cano had a giant one building between his eyes. With record heat expected, he anticipated it could only get worse. He wondered if one of the ladies had some aspirin in her purse.

He was turning to ask for some from Officer Janice Henley when he spotted two strangers standing in the entryway. He typed them immediately. *Great,* he swore to himself, *a plain Jane and her queen escort. Just what we need.*

He made his way across the room, dodging federal agents, his boss, and various desks and chairs to meet them.

The plain Jane stuck out her hand and said, "Officer Cano? I'm Clarissa Wright and this is my friend Irving Waverly. You asked us to come here to help you with the missing Mayor case."

Officer Cano took her hand and gave it a good shake and motioned for them to step into a side office. He closed the door behind them.

"Right." He looked at them sharply. "We've had some developments."

Rissa's eyebrows shot up.

Cano clarified. "There are federal agents involved now. It complicates things." His head pounded like someone was taking a wooden mallet to his skull. "I've talked to the chief of police and he can spare one man to assist you in your . . . search."

Before they could say anything, Officer Cano opened the door and called out, "Jimmy!"

A young man, grinning, came over. To Rissa, he looked not a day over seventeen. His police uniform, too large for his thin frame, bunched up where his belt kept it from falling off. He had traces of acne on his forehead and the buzz cut on his light red hair looked fresh. As he came toward them, he banged his belt-slung pistol on a desk. Cano winced.

"This is Officer Jimmy Reyes-Smith."

"Smith-Reyes, sir," corrected Officer Jimmy.

Cano frowned. "Right. Sorry." He motioned to the pair standing in front of him. "These are the people I told you about, Officer *Smith-Reyes*, and I need you to help them like we talked about, OK?"

The young officer grinned and nodded his head.

Officer Cano continued. "Take an unmarked car – the brown Ford would work – a radio, and a map. This lady says she thinks she can find the Mayor."

Rissa swallowed.

Officer Jimmy turned to lead them to the brown Ford.

Officer Cano grabbed him by the arm. "And Jimmy," he said directly into the young man's face, "no heroics. If you *do* find something," the doubt was heavy in his voice, "call for backup. Don't try anything on your own."

Officer Jimmy smiled, nodded, and led the bewildered pair outside.

Officer Cano watched them disappear around the corner as they headed toward the staff parking lot.

God help us all, he thought.

CHAPTER 36

Walking to the car, Rissa could feel rivulets of sweat roll down her back. The young police officer had stopped to pick up large, cold bottles of water for each of them; Rissa held hers against her cheek. She could tell it would be a long, hot day.

"Officer . . . ?" She couldn't remember if it was Smith-Reyes or Reyes-Smith.

"You can call me Officer Jimmy. Poor Officer Cano can never remember my last name, and this makes it easier. More friendly." He grinned at her. She noticed he had light apricot-colored freckles on his nose and cheeks.

"Well, you can call me Rissa. It's short for Clarissa, but most people call me Rissa." She motioned to Trey. "This is my friend Irving Waverly the third."

Trey stuck out his hand. "Please call me Trey," he said. Officer Jimmy shook his hand and nodded.

Rissa touched Trey's shoulder. "You sit in front, since you've got longer legs." They all got in the car and Officer

Jimmy started it, turning the air conditioner on high. Trey spread out their Arizona map.

"I think we want to start here," Trey said, pointing to the Four Peaks wilderness area east of the Phoenix metropolitan area.

Officer Smith-Reyes nodded. "What are we looking for?"

Rissa hesitated. "We're looking for the Mayor." *Silly question*, she thought. "I think it has something to do with that area. And are there bighorn sheep in this state?"

"Yes, ma'am, we have desert bighorns. They'll be a bit lower to be near the water this time of year. You see them sometimes on the eastern end of the Apache Trail and in other remote wilderness areas." Officer Jimmy sucked on his lower lip for a second. "I meant, what sort of clues are we looking for? My grandfather on my mother's side sometimes could find things that were lost, and he told me he did it by paying attention to clues he got in his head." Officer Jimmy's eyes were distant. "He could levitate tables, too."

Rissa wasn't sure who was more crazy at this point, she or the young policeman, but she decided that she'd better follow through since they'd come all this way.

Trey offered, "Well, Rissa was telling me that she had a dream in which she saw a horse with a big saddle on it, but the horse disappeared behind her, after which she saw a mountain range with four peaks in it, and then she saw a bighorn sheep with two horns that fused into one and sank into the ground. Those are the clues we're working with right now. I'm sure she'll get more when the time arises."

No pressure there, Rissa thought.

Officer Jimmy ruminated on this. "Well, there's Horse Mesa dam up on Apache Lake as you get near the Four Peaks area, and if we put that behind us, we'll be traveling east where we might see some bighorn sheep." His finger made a circle on the map. "We'll be traveling the Apache Trail loop, around the Superstitions here."

"What are the Superstitions?"

"The Superstition Mountains. That's where there's supposed to be the Lost Dutchman's Mine. Old Jacob Waltz supposedly found a gold mine there, but he died over a hundred years ago, never telling anybody where it was. They've been looking for the mine ever since. I think that's where the Superstitions got their name." He nodded and smacked his lips. "Yep, you could find yourself a good hiding place up there in the Superstitions." He looked at Rissa through the rear-view mirror. "It seems like as good a place as any to start."

CHAPTER 37

It took over an hour to reach the turnoff to the Apache Trail. Officer Jimmy decided to go northeast first, taking the clockwise loop around the Superstition Wilderness area. Rissa was feeling light-headed, having lost three hours in the time change from Honolulu to Phoenix, and she realized she'd forgotten to eat breakfast. She wondered if the young policeman could hear her stomach rumbling from the back seat.

She took a gulp of water from her water bottle and forced herself to concentrate. She looked at the rugged landscape, with huge boulders strewn about as if a giant had thrown them sidelong from a great height, and at the scraggly shrubs and prickly pear scattered on the desert floor. She searched for clues, any hints of recognition in her subconscious mind. Not feeling any, she continued looking out the window with a glum face.

Officer Jimmy was telling Trey about the various points of interest in the area. He pointed to an area off to their right, where a sign marked the entrance to the Lost Dutchman State

Park. He pointed at Superstition Mountain, which loomed like a monolith over the area below it. It was beautiful, Rissa acknowledged, but not what she was looking for.

A few miles later, their uniformed tour guide told them, was Canyon Lake. Its sapphire blue waters contrasted with the dry, dusty brown terrain around it. The rocky landscape with the saguaro and prickly-pear cacti, some stick-like plants with tiny, mint-shaped leaves that Officer Jimmy called ocotillo, spiky agaves and desiccated creosote bushes gave the area a desolate, forbidding air. Officer Jimmy explained that the unusual rock formations were made of volcanic ash and basalt. "But no need to worry – none of the volcanoes here are active anymore," he added with a laugh. They crossed over two onc-lane bridges, which made Rissa hold her breath as she willed herself to stare straight ahead.

A bit further down the curvy mountain road, a sign told them that they had arrived in the town of Tortilla Flat, population 6. Officer Jimmy slowed the car.

"Hungry?" he asked as he parked the vehicle.

The town consisted of two large buildings side by side, and one smaller one, which looked like an old, one-room schoolhouse, further down the road. It was like stepping into a movie set for an old Western; the façades of the two larger buildings were constructed with vertical slats of boards, faded and weathered by the hot climate. Rissa half expected to see horses tied to the hitching posts that bordered the wooden walkways in front of the buildings. She read the signs near the roofline – one building was marked "Livery Stable" and the other "Superstition Saloon." They jumped out of the car and headed for the saloon. A large, wooden Indian stood near the door, much of its paint worn away. Inside, the Western theme continued. The saloon section featured a bar where, instead of bar stools, a row of Western saddles served as seats. Rissa glanced at Trey. He raised his eyebrows.

"Well, Rissa, are these the saddles from your dream?" he asked.

"No, different shape," she replied, as they were ushered to a table in the restaurant section.

It took a minute for Rissa to notice that the walls were covered with one dollar bills. Each donor had scrawled their name and home town over Washington's face before someone stapled the bill onto the wall. Every few yards, a handmade sign proclaimed, "Do not steal the wallpaper."

Rissa was famished, but decided on a sandwich with a salad and a tall glass of iced tea. About halfway through her sandwich, her hunger was staved off enough to ask the young officer some questions that had just occurred to her.

"So, Officer Jimmy, I've been meaning to ask you – was there a letter delivered with the Mayor's finger? A ransom note or something?" She realized, after having asked him, that this was hardly mealtime conversation.

It didn't faze him. He batted his pale eyelashes and said, "Yes, ma'am, it was a letter stating that his life was in danger if we didn't deliver a hundred thousand dollars in unmarked bills in a brown briefcase."

Trey's face showed interest. "Where was it to be delivered? That may have a bearing on where he's being held."

"Oh, yes, sir, it could. Hadn't thought of that." He squinted. "I believe it said it was to be delivered at the base of the airplane at Bonsall Park in west Phoenix. Or is it south Glendale? It's pretty close in there."

"An airplane?" Trey asked.

"Yeah, I think it came from the old Litchfield Naval Air Facility in Goodyear, in the far west Valley. Anyway, he, she, or they want the briefcase at the base of the frame that holds up the airplane by midnight."

Rissa nearly choked. "When?"

"Midnight, tonight," Officer Jimmy replied.

CHAPTER 38

Around five miles out of Tortilla Flat, the pavement ended, slowing their progress. The brown Ford kicked up pebbles and dust and the heat made everyone sleepy after their filling lunch. Rissa could feel the sweat pooling between her shoulder blades and under her thighs. She moved to the center of the back seat to feel the blast of the air conditioning.

"Um, Officer Jimmy, how long before we reach the Horse dam?" she asked. Time was feeling very precious.

He grinned at her in the rearview mirror. "Well, ma'am, after we get up this hill, we've got maybe ten miles – maybe a little more. Then we'll be seeing Apache Lake and Horse Mesa Dam, along with Four Peaks in the distance."

Trey studied the map. "Just how long is the whole Apache Trail?"

"Well, sir, I'm not sure, but I think it's over a hundred and twenty miles – just the loop. The distance from the station to the beginning of the Trail is another, oh, fifty-plus miles."

Rissa looked at her watch. It was already past noon. A little over eleven hours to find this person. Her body was anxious to get out of the heat, and her soul felt an urgency to complete her task. But what was she looking for? Her eyes scanned the horizon, but nothing spoke to her.

Just beyond the crest of the hill they began to see the deep blue of Apache Lake. In the distance, a mountain range with four distinct summits peeked through the summer haze. Above them, a couple of turkey vultures flew in wide circles, scanning the horizon for their next meal. Officer Jimmy braked the car to a halt.

Three sets of eyes searched the land beyond. It was rough terrain, and Rissa hoped that they wouldn't have to start searching on foot. She looked at her feet and remembered that she was still wearing her casual sandals from her trip to Hawaii; they would not help her in climbing the rocky footholds or protect her from the patches of prickly pear and other cactus plants and thorny shrubs she couldn't name. She moved to the left side of the car to get a better look. There were enough canyons and gullies, plus boulders and rocky outcroppings, to hide an army. She felt a growing sense of panic in the pit of her stomach. *This just doesn't feel right*, she thought.

Officer Jimmy studied her in the rearview mirror. He wanted to give her enough time to get her bearings.

Trey cleared his throat. "What do you think, Rissa?"

Her eyes continued their search. "I -- I -- don't know. It just doesn't look right. The Four Peaks aren't the same shape I saw, and I really don't know if they were symbolic anyway, you know, of the number four." Officer Jimmy's eyebrows arched in the mirror's reflection. "And the lake doesn't feel right." She motioned to the whole area before them. "It's just so big, and so rocky, and so hilly – I just can't say it's here." She sighed with frustration.

"That's OK, ma'am, perhaps if we drove a little further, you might feel differently. Just keep looking. Tell me if you want me to stop or anything." Officer Jimmy eased the car back into motion. The sound of pebbles crunching under the wheels, along with the roar of the air conditioner on its highest setting made more conversation difficult.

They continued several more slow miles in silence. Trey kept track of their position with his finger on the map and Rissa kept moving from window to window, searching the landscape for shapes or images she recognized.

The Horse Mesa Dam is behind us. I've seen the Four Peaks. Where are the bighorn sheep? Rissa's mind circled around and around. *Am I crazy? Is there something I'm missing?* She felt the tension and frustration build. *This isn't helping anyone,* she told herself. She started counting her breaths to calm herself down. After a few minutes, her breaths grew deeper and slower, and her mind felt clearer.

Over a half hour later, they reached another, larger lake. They could see a few boaters on the blue waters, brave people who were willing to endure the intense afternoon heat.

"Roosevelt Lake," offered Officer Jimmy, "the largest lake within Arizona."

Trey unfolded the map to look. "I would have thought that Lake Powell was larger, but it's mostly in Utah, isn't it?"

Officer Jimmy nodded.

Rissa leaned over the front seat. "Say, could we stop at a rest area or something? I need to splash some water on my face."

A couple of miles further, Officer Jimmy parked the car and Rissa got out. The car had been hot, with the heat permeating the windows and floorboards, but Rissa's first step into the open was a reminder of how punishing the desert temperatures could be. The sun beat on her without mercy. It baked the top of her head, it was reflected off the pavement and the rocks, and the dryness of the air sucked the moisture from her mouth. *I hope the Mayor isn't out here in this*, she thought. *He'd never survive.* The air throbbed with the raspy call of cicadas. Flying insects zoomed over dry bushes and through scraggly trees, making snapping sounds as they flew by. The pavement underneath her feet felt squishy, as if it were melting. She spotted the restroom and moved there with hasty steps.

She used the facilities, washed her hands, and rinsed her face. She looked in the dirty mirror, willed herself into a relaxed state and closed her eyes. *I need some help here*, she prayed. *Give me a sign, or give me some wisdom. Please.*

She looked at herself again and, in the dusty haze that coated the mirror, visually traced the outline of her head in the reflection. She played with letting her eyes go in and out of focus. *Is it a head, or is it a rock? Is it a head, or is it a balloon? Is it a head at all?* She felt a little giddy.

Let go of what you think you are supposed to see, Rissa, and you will see more clearly.

She stood there a couple of minutes, letting the message permeate her core. Outside, the only things she could hear were the idling of the car, the droning cicadas, and the shrill sounds the flying insects made as they shot past the building.

She returned to the car, singing softly to herself. "Shoo, fly, don't bother me, shoo, fly, don't bother me, shoo, fly, don't bother me, for I belong to somebody."

CHAPTER 39

Rissa slid back into the back seat of the car and announced, "We need to go back to the area around Henderson. We're nowhere near the right place." She felt sure about this, the first thing she'd felt sure about since they'd landed in Phoenix.

Officer Jimmy said a quiet, "Yes, ma'am," as he turned onto the road leading to Globe and back to U.S. 60. The road was paved, but still winding and narrow. He drove as fast as he safely could.

Trey turned to look at her and opened his mouth to say something, but shut it again. He offered her a soft smile instead.

Rissa settled herself in the center of the back seat again, enjoying the blast of cool air from the car's air conditioner. She closed her eyes and let her mind relax.

She imagined her twin soul being held captive somewhere. She wondered if he could sense her thoughts. She had sensed his feelings on occasion in the past, she remembered. *After all, since physical twins sometimes hear each other's thoughts, or feel each other's feelings, why not spiritual twins?* She focused her mind and set her intention to send a message.

Hold on, we're coming to find you.

CHAPTER 40

The boy called Peter seemed agitated. He muttered to himself, paced on the wooden floor of the shack, and kept looking at the watch he'd taken from David's wrist and strapped on his own. David, lying on his side, was tired of the boy's footsteps causing the floorboards to slap his face and body. He grunted to get his attention and fixed his eyes on the two remaining gallon-sized containers of water.

"Thirsty, eh?" asked Peter.

David nodded. He wanted to be moved out of this position and to stretch his legs and shoulders. Some water would help, too.

"Probably a good idea. I'll be leaving soon and don't know when I'll be back." Peter moved to loosen the cord tying David's wrists and ankles together. He lifted David up into a sitting position and put his back against a wall.

"Hungry?" Peter yanked the filthy sock from David's mouth. David spat out dirt and dust.

"Yes, please," he croaked. His mouth felt as dry and dusty as the Sahara.

Peter poured water into his mouth. David swallowed and could feel his tissues expanding with the hydration, like a wilted plant coming back to life. He drank as much as Peter would allow him.

Peter then fed him the remaining crackers and jerky. David wondered if it were wise he ate the last bit of food. He wasn't sure when he might eat again.

"More water, please?" David asked. His voice sounded stronger.

"Sure. Just don't drink so much you have to pee, 'cuz I won't be here to help you with that." Peter laughed.

David gulped a bit more and sighed. He caught Peter's eye.

"Where are you going?" he asked in a gentle voice.

"I'm going to find us both a ticket out of here. A ticket marked freedom for you," he said, putting the cap back on the water jug and setting it aside, "and a ticket marked moolah for me." He laughed at his own joke.

"What do you need the money for? I know some people who could help you."

Peter's mood turned violent in a split second. With the swift motion of a rattlesnake, he grabbed the knife from his pocket, flicked it open and pointed it at David's throat. His breath came in jagged bursts as he pressed his sweaty face in front of David's.

"Look, I don't need your kind of help. I've got my family, and I've seen too much of what you people do to my kind." He pressed the knife so that David winced. "I'm the man of the family now, and I'm going to do what I can to provide for them." He held his stare an extra second to get his point across, closed the knife with a click, slid it into his pocket and backed away.

David nodded and lowered his head. He didn't want to further anger the young man. He waited a couple of minutes for the tension to ease.

"I can see you want to help your family very much. It must be a lot of responsibility."

Peter turned and nodded. "Yeah, well, a guy's gotta do what he's gotta do."

"I understand. It must be very hard figuring out what to do, especially for someone who's still pretty young."

The boy puffed out his chest and gave it a thump. "Yeah, well, I'm Peter, remember? The Rock. I can handle it."

"Yes, I know you're tough. And smart, too. It just makes me sad, seeing someone have to carry such a heavy load when he should be out there having fun." David studied the young man's face.

Peter turned to look out the doorway. He stared into the distance, surveying the cloudless sky.

"Yeah, well, life really sucks sometimes. That's lesson number one." His voice betrayed an anger borne of at least three generations of betrayal, neglect, and violence.

David let the silence in the stifling hot shack absorb Peter's words.

He lowered his voice. "I think the worst part of life is thinking that you have to handle it all alone."

Peter turned to him, his face a stone. "Well, that's where I think you're wrong. We're born alone, we die alone, and what we do with the stuff in between is what makes us or breaks us. And *I*'m not going to let it break *me*." With that, he picked up the sock from the floor, shook it once, stuffed it into David's mouth, rolled him back onto his side and lashed his wrists to his ankles. He gave the ties one last test with a harsh yank.

In three strides, he was out the door.

CHAPTER 41

"Jeez, Rissa, will you stop it with that song?" Trey sounded exasperated. Whether it was from her humming about shooing flies or from the starts and stops of rush-hour traffic of downtown Phoenix, Rissa couldn't tell.

"Sorry. I didn't know you could hear me," she said.

Officer Jimmy peered at her from the rear view mirror. "It'll be about dinner time by the time we get back to the station and the end of my shift for today." He paused as he edged around a long line of cars that were in the I-17 turnoff lane. "But I'd be happy to drive you around again after I go home to let out the dogs and check on my grandmother."

Rissa wondered if the young officer lived with his grandmother. From his unusual lack of self-absorption, suggesting that he was accustomed to focus on others first, she wouldn't be surprised.

"That would be great. May we treat you to dinner?" Rissa hoped that her meager resources could accommodate him.

"Thanks, ma'am, but my grandmother will have dinner waiting for me." He paused and Rissa could see his face redden underneath his freckles. "I'd invite you over, but she doesn't do well with surprises."

"That's understandable. We'll grab something and meet you wherever is convenient," said Trey. "Where do you live, and could we meet you somewhere near there?"

"I live in Willis, west of Buckeye. It's just further down I-10." He thought a minute. "How about if I just drop you off downtown and you can catch a bite and then I'll pick you up in, say, an hour?"

Trey and Rissa agreed, and it was half past six when they escaped the confines of city traffic and were making their way toward Willis. Rissa perked up when they entered the town. Her eyes scanned each building as if she were searching for something. *"Downtown" is a bit of an exaggeration*, she thought. They passed a truck stop with a half dozen semitrailers parked in the large lot behind, a small grocery store, and a tiny fast food stand. A couple of homes with citrus trees in their yards were across the street. A pair of curly-tailed dogs trotted down the road. In the distance, she could see more homes surrounded by acreage. She couldn't tell what they were growing. Corn or sorghum, she guessed.

Officer Jimmy dropped them off at the truck stop, assuring them that it served "good grub," and drove off. They stood there, blinking at each other.

Rissa felt light-headed from the lack of sleep and the oppressive heat. She smiled at Trey and said, "You know, I think you look a little wrinkled."

He playfully pushed her shoulder and opened the door to the restaurant. "After you, my dear," he said with a mock bow.

The waitress, coffee pot in hand, waved them in and said in a loud voice, "Sit yerself." In spite of all the sitting she had done that day, Rissa was glad to collapse on the lumpy, red vinyl seat of the booth underneath a ceiling fan. A jukebox in the corner blared an old country-western song and weary truckers ate their burgers and fries in silence.

Rissa saw the look of distaste on Trey's face and laughed. "Hey, this is just the Arizona version of Lenny's Fish Hut."

"Well, all I can say is, they better have 'good grub'," said Trey with a sniff.

The waitress rushed by and slapped two paper menus on the table. "Be back in a sec," she said.

Rissa picked up one of the menus. It was printed on one long sheet of paper that had small, square ads framing the menu listings. Rissa looked at the ads with mild interest through her tired eyes. Betsy's Bar and Grill, Buckeye. Tony's Garage, Avondale – "We can fix your car, truck, or RV." A Best Western Hotel in Goodyear. And in the lower right hand corner, an ad for an RV park. Rissa squinted. There was an outline of a double-peaked mountain above the name. The left peak was high and pointed, and the right peak was taller but more block in shape. In between a pronounced curve, like the bottom portion of a U, connected the two peaks. Underneath, the caption read, "Saddle Mountain RV Resort, Tonopah."

"Oh, my God," gasped Rissa.

Trey looked up from his menu. "What is it?" he asked.

"I recognize this shape." She pointed to the ad on her menu. "Saddle Mountain. Like in my dream. It's not a horse we're looking for, but the saddle." She cradled her forehead in her left hand, staring at the ad. "We're near the right place."

CHAPTER 42

At the same time, a small silver Nissan drove down the highway past Willis, heading east toward Phoenix. Rigoberto was whistling, partly to distract himself from the heat, and partly in anticipation of his expected bounty. *I'll be rich after tonight*, he thought.

He drove in the slow lane, traveling just under the speed limit. He didn't want to risk catching the attention of the Highway Patrol. During a trip to Tonopah that morning, he'd exchanged the license plate on the Nissan with one he'd stolen from an old junker he'd found. The plate was expired, so he smeared it with mud as best he could and hoped that nobody would take too close a look.

It took over an hour at that speed to travel from his hideaway in the desert to Bonsall Park in Glendale. He circled the tree-filled park a couple of times, which took a while because of heavy traffic, and finally parked across the street and up a block in front of a busy strip mall. He chose a space that faced the green oasis.

Rigo stayed in his car, surveying the park for a few minutes. The center of the park featured a man-made lake, where people often came to feed the ducks that paddled in the murky water or to enjoy a picnic in the shade. Few people were there now, because of the oppressive heat even in this last hour before twilight. He studied the area around the airplane, a green and tan Super Sabre, held permanently in a take-off angle on a silver stand. The airplane was across the street, just north of the park itself, in an area that was devoid of much vegetation except for a sparse lawn. He smiled at his plan. It was open enough for him to see if there was anyone waiting for him, and yet busy enough so he could remain hidden.

His stomach growled. He decided he could spare a couple of dollars for a quick bite at the Burger Grill on the northwest corner, located diagonally from the park. He scanned the parking lot, and saw mostly pickup trucks, some with open trailers hauling yard clippings, palm leaves and tree branches, as well as a few beat-up sedans, a couple with cracked windshields, and one with a straightened wire hanger in place of its antenna. No police cars in sight. He looked at his clothing and glanced at his sweaty face in the mirror. He smoothed down his hair, and decided that his appearance would fit in with the weary yard workers who were eating inside.

He went in the restaurant and ordered a burger and large cola. He sat in the corner of the dining room, away from the noise at the counter. He needed to think.

Part one of the plan is already in place, he told himself. *Now, for part two.*

As his brain considered the possibilities, he chewed slowly and made himself small. *No need to attract attention here*, he reasoned. *I can be patient.*

He felt like a spider weaving its web. He'd heard the news reports during his jaunt that morning. He knew that the police were taking him seriously. It made him feel strong and tall inside.

If all went according to plan, in less than six hours he would be a richer man.

And if it didn't go according to plan, he thought, *I could be a killer.*

CHAPTER 43

Officer Jimmy came striding in the truck stop restaurant, scanned the room, and headed with quick steps toward Rissa and Trey's table. Rissa noticed that, this time, he didn't hit any tables with the gun slung at his waist.

He spoke just above a whisper. "We have to go. Now." Beads of sweat mixed with the freckles on his face.

"What's going on?" Rissa was alarmed by the urgency in his voice. She and Trey had just been served their meals and she felt regret that they might have to leave their food uneaten. She was hungry and tired from the long day.

"The Chief called. He said that since I have the only unmarked car that isn't in the shop, I need to come in to assist in the stake-out in Glendale." He shifted uncomfortably on his feet. "And he wants you two to come along."

Trey motioned to the waitress to come and wrap up their dinners as he took out a few bills from his wallet to leave on the table. The woman's flustered air proved to be only a mask for her quick efficiency, earned from years of repetition.

Rissa and Trey followed Officer Jimmy out the door, both with a sack of food and a large Styrofoam cup in hand.

Trey sat in the front passenger seat, and Rissa in the back as before. She stuffed a heavily salted French fry in her mouth, chewed, and asked, "Why did the Chief want us to come along?"

Officer Jimmy's ears reddened. "Uh, well, it seems that he's more than a little disappointed that we didn't have any results after all that driving today," he stammered, "and he's also tired of the Feds treating him and his department like they were a bunch of know-nothings." He swallowed. "The Chief is hoping you can help him out by making him look good."

Trey pursed his lips. "That seems to be a bit of change since this morning. I didn't think they took us seriously at all."

"Well, I guess it's been a tense day and the Chief is grabbing at straws to assist his department." The younger policeman's neck turned a deep pink. "Uh, I didn't mean any offense in that."

"None taken, right, Rissa?" Trey laughed. It was the first time he'd laughed in many hours. Rissa, her mouth full, shook her head.

After a few miles of silence while Rissa and Trey finished their meals, Rissa took a big sip on her cola, put her meal wrappings back in their sack, brushed the crumbs off her lap and said, "Trey, could I look at the map again?"

Trey wiped his mouth with regal flourish and spread the map out on his lap. Rissa perched over his seat back. "Where's Tonopah?"

Trey pointed with a long finger. "Here, off I-10, a bit west of where we were eating dinner."

"And where's Saddle Mountain?"

Trey frowned as he searched. "It's not on this map."

Officer Jimmy piped up, "Saddle Mountain? That's just a little west of Tonopah. Not too far, really. I used to hunt rabbits there with my grandfather when I was a kid."

Rissa studied the youthful face of the young officer and tried not to let her amusement show.

"Well, Officer Jimmy, I think that's where we need to go when we start searching for the Mayor." She felt a pang of impatience that they were headed in the opposite direction from there.

"Well, the Chief ordered us to try to find his kidnapper first. They expect him or her to be waiting for their payoff in Bonsall Park at midnight. We need to be there long before to check out the area and find a good place to observe without being too conspicuous."

"I understand," said Rissa with a sigh. The motion of the car, along with the contentment of a full stomach, made her sleepy. She wondered how long it would be before she would sleep in a real bed again.

She did not take long to think it through, for, in minutes, she was asleep.

CHAPTER 44

The crackle of the police radio woke her up. Rissa opened her eyes to see that they were parked in a large, busy parking lot in front of a strip mall. The Ford was pointed with its front end facing east, toward the main street. Across the street was a two-seater jet airplane, frozen in take-off position on a silver stand.

"Yes, we're in position," affirmed Officer Jimmy into the radio hand set.

"Do not make any further radio contact unless you have something definite, understood?" The voice sounded tense through all the static.

"Yes, sir," responded Officer Jimmy, who put the hand set back onto the face of the radio. He sighed. This was going to be a long evening.

"What do we do now?" asked Rissa.

"We wait, and keep our eyes open." He glanced at Trey, who was still slumbering, his head propped up by the door frame. He lowered his voice. "You're supposed to let me know if you sense something definite."

"OK. I'll do what I can. This is all new to me, you know."

Officer Jimmy nodded. "My grandfather used to find things for people all the time, but he said anyone could pick up information with their sixth sense if they wanted to."

"Did he teach you how?"

"Well, he tried, but I thought it was kind of silly at the time. I wanted results right away, and when I didn't get what I wanted, I quit trying, I guess."

Rissa nodded.

"I remember my grandfather told me to step back in my mind and imagine a viewing screen, like in a movie theater. He said if you waited long enough without trying to imagine anything yourself, the images would come up and you'd see what you needed to see." He shrugged. "Something like that, anyway. It never really worked for me, but then, I didn't know how to slow down my mind. It's always going a mile a minute."

"I know what you mean," Rissa said. "I find that focusing on my breathing helps, and imagining going down a staircase helps me calm down and relax my mind. There are different tricks I've read about." She shrugged.

"Anyway, ma'am, if you want to just sit and relax and see what comes, I'll sit quietly."

Rissa nodded and closed her eyes. She counted her breaths, from one to four, over and over, for a few minutes. Feeling more present, she imagined herself going down a series of steps. *Ten, nine, eight, more and more relaxed, seven, six, five.* She was on a small landing and took a minute to feel her level of relaxation. *Even deeper still*, she told herself. *Four, three, two, deeper yet, and one.* She was in a beautiful corridor and she offered a prayer to her spirit guides for assistance. *Please show me who we're looking for. Help us save the Mayor,* she prayed. She felt herself being led down the hallway to a room on her left. She entered in and saw a large screen; facing it was a large, overstuffed chair. She sat. The screen was blank. She waited. She focused on her inhaling and exhaling, letting her thoughts pass like clouds in a windy sky.

For a long time, the screen in front of her was blank, like a TV showing a dark, snowy picture. The thought crossed her mind that perhaps she wouldn't have any more success than Officer Jimmy, but she decided to stay with it. *Relax, and let go.*

After a while, she noticed that the bottom left corner of the screen had cleared up. She noticed without forcing any meaning onto it. It was a small foot, the sole of a child who was crawling. The picture opened up further and she noticed a messy floor, with piles of papers and soda cans strewn about. The child was crawling toward an overfilled garbage can. Flies buzzed in the air and what appeared to be a kitchen beyond the child grew more distinct in her mind. She heard in her mind a TV blaring, and saw a woman's foot with toenails painted a bright red. Her vision followed up the calves of the woman. She saw sores, some scabbed over and some open and red, on the woman's legs. Above that, a loose green dress with orange flowers draped over the woman's knees. She looked up at the woman's head, which was just coming into focus. An odd shade of red hair, and a puffy, pale face. Rissa felt a flicker of recognition. *I've been here before*, she thought. She let herself continue to follow the vision. The woman was yelling. Off to the right, a man, dark-haired with a deeply tanned face, yelled back at the woman. Rissa did not know the man. The man's face grew red with anger as he raised his fist. The woman screamed and backed into the kitchen. The man followed. Rissa's vision shifted so that she felt she were a third person, standing between the screaming adults. The man's focus changed so that he was looking at Rissa, who realized she was seeing through another person's eyes. His raised fist came down hard onto the person whose mind Rissa was seeing through. She felt herself being struck, over and over, in the shoulders, the stomach, the back. She felt herself crumple onto the floor, but the blows kept coming. She curled up and grew cold and distant inside. Rissa understood that this was how this person survived the abuse. After a while, the screen went blank. Rissa let the feelings go. The experience so affected her that she felt physically paralyzed – she doubted she could raise a finger. She rested a while.

Then, the thought came. *I know who this is.*

CHAPTER 45

Rissa awoke when she felt a hand gently tapping her knee. "Hey, Rissa, wake up," Trey's voice said.

She struggled to open her eyes. Although the parking lot was well lit, she could see that it was night. She took in a deep breath and said, "I'm sorry, I must have fallen asleep."

Officer Jimmy smiled at her through the rearview mirror. "That's all right, ma'am."

"What time is it?" she asked with a yawn.

"A little before midnight."

Rissa snapped awake. "Goodness! I was out that long?" The fog cleared in her mind and she remembered her vision in detail. "Look, I think I know who our kidnapper is."

Both men turned around in their seats to face Rissa.

"You'll need to contact the Department for the Protection of Children in Denver, but his last name is Saenz. Roberto, Ricardo, something like that. I think he's still only a teenager. He's living with his grandmother here in Phoenix. He came here last spring to get away from the abuse at home." She flushed. "I hope that helps."

"Do you have a physical description?" asked Officer Jimmy, who was reaching for the radio.

"No. But there's a photo of him in his mother's apartment. I remember seeing it." The memory pained her. "If she's still alive."

Officer Jimmy relayed the information Rissa gave him over the radio. The static on the radio could not mask the surprise in the Chief's voice.

Trey turned around to face her as the young policeman spoke into the radio. "Good job, Rissa," he whispered, a hint of a smile on his weary face.

Rissa considered for a minute and shook her head. "We still have to find the Mayor," she said.

CHAPTER 46

Rigoberto sat two blocks away. He had dawdled over his meal and sat in the restaurant, watching the people and cars in the parking lot outside. He noticed that around sundown, a few dark, shiny sedans started to circle the block around Bonsall Park and one parked across the street from the airplane. The people inside did not leave their cars, but left them running with the air-conditioning on. Most of the cars had tinted windows, so Rigo could not see who was sitting inside, but one car, a dusty brown Ford, had three people in it. One of them, who looked like a boy not much older than himself, was in the driver's seat. He had reddish hair, cut short in military style. Next to him was a much taller man, with blond hair cut in an expensive style. *Not many natural blonds or redheads in this neighborhood*, Rigo thought. He felt a surge of pride that his actions garnered so much attention. Behind the two men sat a young woman, probably in her early 20s, with straight, brown hair tied in a ponytail that fell below her shoulders. She looked like she was sleeping.

Time for the second part of my plan, he decided.

With nonchalance, he left the restaurant and got into the silver Nissan. He smirked that the people in the sedans were so focused on the park that they completely ignored him in his stolen car. He drove two blocks south and parked on a side street, in front of an apartment complex.

He knew from living in a series of apartments throughout his life that they were rarely quiet places. The adults who worked often had to take two or more low-paying jobs just to make ends meet, and that left the kids largely unsupervised. He remembered that as a child, he would ride his bike in the middle of the complex at one or two in the morning because his mother was passed out drunk and his father was either working an odd job or asleep from exhaustion. And he remembered that he was not the only child who enjoyed the freedom that night brought.

Rigo waited, and spotted a couple of boys, probably brothers, who were throwing a baseball at each other on a patch of weedy lawn near the edge of the complex. He watched them a short while, moving closer and closer so that they could see him, and see that he was enjoying their game. His short stature and the darkness masked his age, and the boys started throwing the ball to him. He played with them in silence for a quarter of an hour. Finally, he caught and held the ball, and walked closer to hand it to them.

"Say, you guys are really good. I bet you're really good at all kinds of sports."

The boys nodded and started to tell him about how they excelled at baseball, football, soccer, and skateboarding.

Rigoberto kept his face looking interested as he listened. "Say, you guys got a bike? I bet you're really fast on that, too."

The boys ran to the stairwell underneath their apartment and pulled out a couple of bicycles.

"You know the airplane across the street from the park?"

The boys nodded.

Rigo flashed his watch at them. "I'm going to time you, one at a time. You ride up to the airplane, do a circle around it, and then come back, and I'll time you to see who is fastest."

The boys laughed with excitement.

"But there's a catch," he continued. "If you see something underneath the airplane, like say, a briefcase or something, you bring it to me, and I'll *give* you this watch."

The boys whooped.

The oldest boy went first and Rigo made a big show of timing him. He returned empty-handed, but Rigo continued the game until each boy had made two runs each.

It was now a quarter to one. He felt a growing sense of anger and betrayal as the boys made yet one more trip each, returning with nothing in their hands. He didn't dare ask the boys to go out again, for fear that they would be stopped by the police who were watching the park and lead them to him. On the last trip, he gave them the watch, much to their delight, and returned to his car.

Rigoberto's stomach churned as he realized that his plan had failed. He was as penniless, and as powerless, as before. He banged his fist on the dashboard and cursed. *What am I going to do now?*

Feeling that the police would be there soon, he drove off, heading south toward I-10.

He pictured the man lying in the shack nearly fifty miles away and pointed the car to take him there. He drove in silence, considering his next steps. As he thought, his hand rubbed the switchblade in his right front pocket, and his insides became as cold and hard as ice.

CHAPTER 47

Rissa, Trey, and Officer Jimmy watched the two boys take turns riding their bikes around the airplane and hurry back down the block.

"How many times have they done that?" asked Trey.

Officer Jimmy hesitated as he reached for the radio speaker. "Um, that's three for the bigger boy, and two for the younger," he said. He pulled his hand away from the radio when he saw a couple of the federal agents' black sedans pull out of the parking lot.

"Here comes the younger boy," noted Rissa. She wondered where his parents were, and if they knew he was riding his bike across busy streets at this late hour.

Off in the distance, they saw the dark sedans cruise down the street and pull to the side of the road. As the younger boy whizzed by, they followed and turned left onto a residential block. Their taillights disappeared into the darkness.

They waited in silence for about ten more minutes. The radio was quiet.

Finally, Officer Jimmy reached for the radio and spoke into the hand set. "Uh, Chief? It's a little past one. Do you still want us to hang around?"

The Chief's voice betrayed his frustration and exhaustion. "No, I think our guy is a no-show. I thought the kids had something to do with all this, but the Feds said they ducked into an apartment complex and disappeared." He sighed. "I guess the kids are a little leery of men in suits driving shiny black sedans. Imagine that." He suppressed a laugh. "Why don't you call it a night? Tell our young lady that we thank her for the information."

"You're welcome," said Rissa. She couldn't let go of the feeling that the Mayor was in more danger than ever and that her work was far from over.

Officer Jimmy hung up the hand set on the radio and turned on the headlights. He was about to put it into gear to back up when Rissa touched his shoulder and said, "Don't go yet."

He put the car back into park and turned around to face her.

Rissa's face flushed. "I need to look at the map again," she said.

Trey spread out the map on his lap and turned on the dome light inside the car. "Can you see OK?" he asked.

Rissa nodded. "Will you point to where Tonopah is again?"

Trey pointed.

"And where is Saddle Mountain?"

Officer Jimmy pursed his lips and pointed to an unmarked mountainous region west of the town. "About there."

Rissa spoke to Officer Jimmy. "I know it has been a really long day for you and all that, but I feel we need to go there, and I feel like it's really important. Are you willing?"

The rearview mirror framed Officer Jimmy's crinkling eyes as he smiled at her. "Yes, ma'am."

"Trey, I need to change places with you. I need to be in front." She hopped out of the car before Trey, in his weary state, could process her words.

They switched places and Rissa spread out the map on her lap. She held her finger on the area Officer Jimmy identified as Saddle Mountain and said, "OK, let's go. And we need to hurry."

CHAPTER 48

As they sped west on I-10, Rissa looked up to admire the bright waxing moon. She guessed that by the following evening, the moon would be at its fullest. A thought struck her. "Hey, Trey, it's the solstice today, isn't it?"

Trey roused himself and said yes. He blinked and admired the queen of the night bestowing her radiance on the desert below. Tomorrow night would be her shortest reign of the year, but with the promise that her authority would grow with each passing night until late in December. The power and promise of the sign of Cancer would be fulfilled. *It is time to return to the power of the feminine*, he thought, as he eyed Rissa's profile in front of him.

Soon, Officer Jimmy took the turn-off for Tonopah. They drove south. Rissa read the street sign. Four hundred and eleventh Avenue. *Four-one-one,* Rissa said to herself. *How funny.*

"How do we get to Saddle Mountain?" she asked.

"Probably the best way is to take the Buckeye-Salome Highway," Officer Jimmy said as he braked to show her on the map with his finger.

"And where does it lead? I'm thinking we're looking for an old hut or small house or something like that. With a wood floor."

Officer Jimmy considered for a moment as he eased the car up to speed. "Well, there are lots of mining claims both on Saddle Mountain and in the mountains north of here." He glanced briefly to stab at the map. "Perhaps there's an old miner's shack somewhere out there."

Rissa turned on the dome light to see the area he had pointed to. As she did so, she noticed that they had passed a small fast-food stand. Above the stand, flying insects buzzed around a small spotlight which illuminated a large hand-painted sign. It read, "Shoo Fly Pies and Sandwiches." Underneath the words was a drawing of a large smiling fly, its wings spread as it perched on a large pie. She recalled the song that had irked Trey all afternoon. "We're on the right track," she announced as they turned northwest onto the Buckeye-Salome Highway.

She picked up the map to bring it closer to her eyes as Officer Jimmy urged the car to go faster on the two-lane road. The mountainous area north of them seemed to have two names. On the east, it was labeled Hummingbird Wilderness. On the west, it was called the Big Horn Wilderness.

"Hurry," she said, touching Officer Jimmy on the shoulder. "I know where he is."

CHAPTER 49

The winds were beginning to blow as Rigoberto edged the silver Nissan onto the jeep trail leading to the old shack. He was relieved to see that the black sedans that followed the kids to the apartment complex had missed his leaving. He had driven I-10 in the slow lane, keeping an eye on his rearview mirror for any sign of the police.

He was driving in total darkness now, illuminated only by the car's headlights and the waxing moon overhead. The creosote bushes and scraggly trees swayed back and forth in the dim light, buffeted by the growing wind storm. In the distance, he could catch the occasional sight of wild eyes reflected in the car's beams.

He pulled the car up to the shack and parked. The winds rocked the car. It would be easy to fall asleep, but he fought the urge. His feeling of betrayal had turned into fierce anger, and he was still toying with a couple of ideas about what to do next.

He got out of the car. The wind slammed the door shut for him. Squinting his eyes to shield them from blowing sand, he walked toward the shack, his right hand resting on the bulge of the switchblade in his pocket.

He walked in, his feet slamming the floorboards, and tore the sock out of the man's mouth. "Your people don't care about you," he stormed.

The man was groggy from the heat and lack of water. "Wha'?" he croaked.

Rigo grabbed the man and jerked him into a sitting position. The man let out a hoarse yell as his legs, tied to his wrists, were bent back into an unnatural position. Rigo let the man go, and the man fell onto his side with a groan.

"I'm telling you, your people don't care about you." He stood over the man, straddling his bent legs.

The man's eyes studied Rigo's face, which was lit by the moonlight that streamed through the cracks between the boards in the walls and ceiling. "They didn't pay up, so now I have to decide what to do with you." He pulled out the switchblade and clicked it open. He waved it in front of the man's eyes. Soft light glinted off its blade.

Rigo pulled the pistol from his waistband. He held it gingerly in his bandaged left hand.

"I'm so sick of you people," Rigoberto was shouting. "You take and take and take and take and you don't care about each other. You don't care about anything but yourself. You don't care about anything but your damn money." He was ranting now, spilling out the anger over the injustice that was his inheritance. He paced the small shack, yelling and waving the weapons before him. The man on the floor held his head up, watching him with sad eyes.

Finally, Rigoberto stopped in front of the man and held up the weapons. Their eyes locked.

In a whisper loud enough to be heard above the wind's blasts outside, Rigo hissed, "So – how do you want to die?"

CHAPTER 50

Officer Jimmy steered the car underneath I-10 as he hurried down the Buckeye-Salome Highway. He reached for the radio handset and flipped the radio on.

"What are you doing?" Rissa asked.

Officer Jimmy pointed to a pair of taillights that flicked off in the distance, partly hidden by a small rise of rocks. "I noticed that car about a mile back. Nobody in their right mind would be taking a joy ride out here at this time of night," he said as he looked at the dusty sky, "or in this weather." He picked up the radio handset. "I'm calling for backup."

He stopped the car, shut off the lights, and made the call. The dispatcher assured him that a nearby highway patrolman could be there in about ten minutes.

He waited a full minute before easing the car back into gear and followed the jeep trail toward where he last saw the taillights. He was glad that the wind would cover the sound of the tires crunching on the stony path.

They rounded the rocky rise and saw a small vehicle parked next to an old wooden shack. They waited a minute to see if they had been heard. Officer Jimmy unsnapped the strap on his holster and pulled the pistol out.

"We can't wait. I've got to go in now," he whispered. He showed Rissa that he needed the dome light covered with her hand as he opened the car door.

He took a step out. He could hear shouting inside the shack. He saw a short man walking back and forth inside. It was the short man who was yelling. Officer Jimmy waited before taking another step. The man continued his rant and seemed focused on something within the shack, totally unaware of his visitors outside.

The short man made another pass in front of the doorway. In the moonlight, Officer Jimmy saw a knife held in his right hand, and another object in his left. Behind him, he heard Trey slide out of the car and shut the car door with a soft click. He took a few more steps toward the shack and motioned for Trey to stay far behind him, out of sight of the man inside.

The wind was fierce now, and the sand stung their faces and eyes. They waited for another roaring blast of the storm and stepped onto the porch. Officer Jimmy positioned himself beside the doorway. Trey edged to a few feet behind him.

With the stealth of an underfed cat, Officer Jimmy peeked around the corner and saw the short man leaning over a dark figure on the floor. The knife's blade glimmered in the pale light.

Officer Jimmy didn't take time to think. He jumped inside the shack and shouted, "Freeze! Police!"

The short man whirled around and threw the knife. It flew like an arrow toward the young officer, missed his face by inches and buried itself, quivering, in a board on the opposite wall. Both Officer Jimmy and Trey crashed in, grappling with the man in the darkness inside.

Outside, Rissa saw the headlights of a car bouncing up the jeep trail behind her. She jumped out of the car. Two policemen got out and ran toward her. "They're inside, and I think he has a weapon," she shouted.

One of the policemen positioned himself a few yards away from the doorway, aiming his pistol at the shack in a two-armed stance. The other jumped onto the small porch and held his body tight against the wall next to the opening. He heard scuffling inside.

A few seconds later, a man stood in the entryway, pointing a pistol at a figure lying on the floor inside. His blond hair gleamed like silver in the moonlight.

"No!" screamed Rissa as she saw the policeman standing near her take aim and fire. The blond man whirled around, grabbed his shoulder where a patch of red was spreading on his shirt, and crumpled outside the doorway.

Rissa ran toward the shack, oblivious to the thorns and stones that cut her feet in their flimsy sandals.

"Trey!" she cried.

She held his head in her arms. His eyes were staring somewhere far away. "No," she sobbed.

Behind her, two more cars pulled up. Four more policemen entered the shack with large flashlights, their guns pulled. Officer Jimmy walked out with a dazed look on his face. One officer held the arm of a lean, short youth, his hands in handcuffs behind him. He led the young man to one of the squad cars. Two more men came to pull Trey away from the shack and onto a makeshift bed they had made for him out of blankets on the ground. Rissa followed and watched him lying there as she wept into her hand. One of the policemen went to his squad car and returned with a medical bag. He put on rubber gloves and put a large, thick bandage on Trey's shoulder, pressing down hard on the wound. Trey groaned. Rissa kneeled on the ground next to him and held his hand.

Officer Jimmy returned to her side and crouched next to her. "They've called for a couple of ambulances. They should be here in a bit," he reassured her.

She noticed another policeman enter the shack with a medical kit in hand.

Rissa asked Officer Jimmy, "The Mayor – is he alive?"

He frowned. "I'm not sure – it was pretty dark and confusing in there – but I think the only one who was shot was our friend Trey here." She nodded.

After what seemed like an eternity, they heard the wail of ambulances on the highway, and soon saw their headlights jumping with every bump on the rough road. A third vehicle, another police car, followed them with lights flashing.

Finally, two more officers emerged from inside the shack and brought out a man with severed bonds hanging from his wrists and ankles. They held him up by his arms, helping him to stand. He was filthy and obviously weak, but Rissa knew who he was. She stood. Her heart recognized him immediately. She searched his face and he looked at her with gentle eyes.

"David!" a woman's voice screamed behind her.

A woman, perhaps thirty years of age, bolted out of the last patrol car to arrive and ran to hold the man in her arms. She was crying, and he rested his head on her shoulders. They stood like that for a long time as the paramedics rolled out the gurney to take him to the hospital.

Rissa stared at the couple, and then at Trey lying on the ground. Her head began to spin. She felt suddenly lost, like her whole world was disappearing with the gusty blasts of the storm. She looked for a lifeline.

She saw an outstretched hand and grabbed it. And so she stood, watching the scene and holding Officer Jimmy's hand as if it were the only thing keeping her from blowing away into the windy night.

CHAPTER 51

Rissa rode with Trey to the hospital and stayed with him until he went into surgery to remove the bullet from his upper chest. A kind nurse cleaned and put ointment and bandages on her feet and legs where she had cut them on the rocks and thorns. As soon as Trey returned from surgery and was placed in a room, she curled up in a chair next to him and slept. Her exhaustion kept her from waking when Trey had the nurses bring in a small bed for her and gently place her on it. She finally awoke a couple of hours before sunset on the longest day of the year.

Trey was still resting, so she snuck into the restroom to inspect the damage from the night's activities. Her face and hair felt gritty from the dust storm. She noticed that someone had brought in her luggage from the rental car and placed it next to the back wall of Trey's room. She searched inside her bag to find some clean clothes, washed up, changed, and decided to walk around. She had some visiting to do.

As she left the room, a slight young man with short red hair approached her. He seemed taller than she remembered, and he walked toward her with confidence in his step.

"Uh, Rissa, ma'am, I'm glad to see you're all right." Officer Jimmy shook her hand and held it for a second.

"Yes, thank you. I was just really tired, but I'm feeling much better after having slept."

"And how's Trey?"

"Sleeping. The doctor said he should be good as new in a couple of days. He lost quite a bit of blood, but there wasn't any major damage to his chest or shoulder." She smiled with relief.

"That's good to hear. The officer who shot him is real broke up about it, so I'll relay the message. Things moved kind of fast last night."

Rissa nodded, replaying the scene in her mind. "I need to ask you – whose gun was it that Trey was holding when he was shot?"

"It belonged to the Mayor, but the Saenz boy had taken it. When we jumped him, Trey grabbed it and pointed it at the boy while I wrestled him to the ground and cuffed him." Officer Jimmy gave a small laugh as he rubbed his chin. "You know, the funny thing is, the gun wasn't loaded."

"What?"

"Yeah, the Mayor kept the gun in his glove compartment for protection, but he hated the idea of guns, so he made sure it was never loaded. He just kept it there for show in case he ever needed to scare off anybody."

"I don't think I'll tell Trey that."

"Well, you take care, ma'am. Good work and thank you for all your help. We couldn't have done it without you."

Rissa grabbed his hand and shook it. "And I want to thank you for believing in me. That meant a lot." She smiled at him. "You know, you're going to be a good policeman. And I predict," she said, with a twinkle in her eye, "that someday soon I'm going to hear good things about *Sergeant* Smith-Reyes, of the Henderson police."

"You'll be the first to know, ma'am," said Officer Jimmy as he waved goodbye and left.

Rissa took a deep breath and walked toward the nurse's station. It was time.

"Excuse me," she asked the nurse on duty. "Could you tell me where the Mayor's room is?"

CHAPTER 52

The sun was setting in pastel hues as the moon rose in all her fullness. The wind had subsided completely, leaving the sky clear of dust and clouds. Rissa returned to Trey's room just as he was starting to eat dinner.

"Can you believe this? Soup and jello. Two of my least favorite things," Trey sniffed.

"Well, eat it to make yourself strong and maybe tomorrow I'll take you back to that truck stop in Willis," teased Rissa.

Trey gave her a withering look and tasted the soup. He added some salt and was soon scraping the bottom of the bowl.

As he ate, Rissa filled him in on what he'd missed. "I met your parents. They flew in early this afternoon and dropped by about an hour ago, but you were sleeping. They've gone now to their hotel, but say they'll be back tomorrow. They were . . ." Rissa searched for the right word, " . . . nice."

"I'll bet they could hardly believe that I would do something so manly as to get shot." He patted his shoulder and winced. "And to have a girl staying in my room, well, I'm sure they think their prayers have been answered." They laughed.

"And both the Chief and Officer Cano came by to offer their thanks. They want us to let them know if there's anything they can do for us while we're here."

"That was . . .nice." Trey smiled.

Rissa grew quiet. "Officer Jimmy came by to say thanks and to wish you well."

Trey searched her face. "OK, spill it, Rissa. Have you met *him*?"

"Who -- 'him'?"

Trey sounded exasperated. "You know who -- *him*."

"You mean the Mayor?"

"Of course! Do tell." He scooped up a quivering slab of green jello, popped it in his mouth, grimaced, and settled in to listen.

"Well, he had surgery about the same time you did to repair his hand where his finger was cut off. They are worried about infection. He's also quite dehydrated and weak."

"I don't want a doctor's report, I want to *hear*! Do you think he's your twin soul or not?"

Rissa continued as if she did not hear him. "And I met his wife. She's really lovely. And she was so thankful for the part we played in his rescue. I didn't tell her everything, of course. He also has two kids, a boy and a girl, about seven and nine, I think."

"Rissa . . ."

"And he's already called the Department of Social Services in Henderson to see what they can do to help out the Saenz boy's grandmother and little brother."

Trey stared at her, frowning.

Rissa heaved a sigh. Her eyes filled with pain. "Trey, I just didn't think he'd be married. That sounds selfish, I know, but I thought being a twin soul with someone meant that you were supposed to be *together*."

Trey looked at her with sympathy. "Come here," he said, patting on the side of his bed while moving his legs to make room for her. He reached over to clasp her hand. "Listen. I think having a twin soul is about something more than the happy endings you see in the movies." He gave her hand a squeeze. "It's about uniting all the dualities – all the twin aspects – within yourself *first*. It's about balancing the male and female essences – the yin and the yang – as well as the mortal and divine parts that exist inside each one of us. At that point, you can help bring balance to your life, to your surroundings, and to the world. God knows this world needs it," he said with a sigh.

"So what's the point of knowing you have a twin soul?"

"I think it may be a reminder that we all have work to do, to bring this balance to ourselves and to the world. I also think it's telling us that we may be ready to move upward and evolve."

Rissa shot him a puzzled look. "What do you mean by that?"

Trey leaned back onto his pillow and considered for a minute. "When I was a boy, my father gave me a kit to create a model of an Egyptian pyramid." He began to talk with his hands, winced, and put his sore left arm down. "Better explain with just one hand," he said with a sheepish grin. "Anyway, think of us all as being a part of the pyramid. We all started as the One, the topmost piece, itself a perfect pyramid. Then, the Big Bang, or something like that, happened, and we scattered into different pieces, like all the different blocks that make up the big pyramid." He stopped for a moment, his face growing more pale.

"And you're saying that our successive lives are about experiencing what it's like to be this block here or that block there within the structure of the pyramid?"

Trey nodded. "But I think when it's time to return to the One, we must join with the closest part of our self, our twin soul, in order to move up. And eventually, that joined self attaches to another, and another, and another, as we move up the pyramid, finally evolving back to the top, to join forever with the One."

Rissa considered for a minute. "But using your pyramid metaphor, we're never apart from the One, because we're always in that great pyramid, just closer or further away from the top, right?" She pursed her lips. "We really are all One."

Trey closed his eyes and smiled. "Well said."

Trey rested a few minutes as Rissa thought in silence. After a bit, with his eyes still closed, he asked, "So, do you know for sure that the Mayor is your twin soul?"

Rissa nodded. "Yes, I knew the minute I heard his voice."

Trey's eyes opened to slits. "You recognized his voice?"

Rissa considered. "No, it's just that . . ." She paused. "Do you know how you describe a man's voice as high or low, or rough or soft or whatever?"

Trey nodded.

"What are you comparing it to?"

Trey's eyes opened completely. "I suppose to some idea of the 'average male voice', or perhaps your own father's voice."

Rissa shook her head. "I would describe my father's voice as rather low, with a rough edge to it." She frowned. "When I heard David's – the Mayor's – voice, I *knew* . . ." Her face began to glow as she continued, "I knew that *his* was the voice that I'd been comparing every other man's voice to, my whole life."

Trey nodded. "It was like going home."

Rissa's eyes filled with tears. "Yes," she whispered.

He reached over and patted her hand. "I know."

Just then, a nurse came in to check Trey's pulse and popped a thermometer into his mouth. Rissa and Trey smiled at each other with shining eyes. After a couple of minutes, the nurse removed the thermometer, frowned, wrote something on his chart, and asked in a sing-song voice, "Time for a pain pill?"

"Most definitely, yes," answered Trey.

The nurse put a capsule in a tiny paper cup, offered it to him with a sip of water, and waited until he swallowed it. Then, she bustled out of the room.

Rissa clasped his hand and asked, "You know, Trey, you never told me who you were waiting for when we first met in Honolulu."

"You remember how I told you I had a twin soul, too, that died in Chicago?"

Rissa nodded.

"Well, the night before you and I met, I had a dream that he was singing at a karaoke club, and kept motioning for me to join him on stage."

"And the place where we met was a karaoke club, wasn't it?"

"Yes, and I thought maybe I could . . ." he searched for the words, "*feel* him more if I went there when it was quiet, if that makes sense."

"And that's where you saw me, dripping wet."

Trey laughed. "Oh, it hurts to laugh," he groaned as he touched his left shoulder. "That's where I saw you, reading one of my favorite books."

"*Wuthering Heights*."

"I waited for a long time to see if I could feel him, and there you were, reading that book, and I figured it was a sign." He nodded. "I guess he led me to you."

"Considering how it turned out," said Rissa, pointing to his shoulder, "maybe that's not such a good thing."

"Oh, stop," said Trey. "Actually, meeting you has helped confirm a lot of things that I've learned about and experienced."

He paused to lick his lips. "I think there may be a book coming out of all this."

"Your theory of everything?"

Trey smiled with closed eyes. The pain pill was making him drowsy. "My theory of ultimate reality, of interconnectedness."

"I look forward to reading it, Professor."

Trey seemed to sleep for a few minutes, but roused and opened his eyes. "What's next, Rissa?"

"Well, I have to leave tomorrow to go back to Denver," she said in a soft voice. "And I have to buy some recordings."

"What?"

"The Mayor – David – said that one of his favorite composers is Brahms, so I better get acquainted with that music so I know what I'm hearing," she said, pointing to her head.

Trey nodded. He took a relaxed breath and asked, "Will you keep in contact with him?"

"You mean, writing, and so forth?"

He nodded.

"Well, I think we have a lot to process right now, so I'll just wait and see." She scratched her forehead and just as her fingers reached to adjust her bangs, she stopped herself and put her hand back in her lap. "I have a lot to keep me busy in Denver. I have my world to heal."

"Understood." He closed his eyes again. "I hear that the University of Denver has a good psychology department."

"I think so. Why?"

"Well, I might want to transfer there sometime. Just think," said Trey with a sly grin, "out-of-state tuition at a private university? It'll cost my parents a *fortune*!"

The next day, Rissa found herself sitting inside a plane bound for Denver. Although she held onto the arm rests with a death grip as she always did on bumpy flights, a slight smile played on her lips. She replayed the events of the last few days in her mind, marveling at the workings of the Universe. She looked out the window and took in the beauty of the changing landscape. Below her, the snow-capped peaks of the Colorado Rockies glistened in the sun. One mountain in particular reminded her of a pyramid. Its summit gleamed like a capstone made of the whitest marble. She recalled Trey's words of the day before. *We are all One*, she affirmed. The plane gave one more jolt as they cleared the last of the turbulence over the mountains. She glanced at her watch.

It read, 11:14.

ABOUT THE AUTHOR

Celina Pavan is an empath, a writer, and works in the fine arts. She and her family of two-leggeds and four-leggeds, along with her enormous collection of books, live in the desert Southwest.

The Gemini Bond is the first of a series.

Visit www.geminisouls.com.